★

IT WOULD HAVE PLEASED TONY TO KNOW HE MADE PAGE ONE OF THE *TIMES*

From the paper Julie learned that Alexander had been shot at close range, apparently with his own revolver, but not by his own hand. His body had been discovered shortly after 11:00 p.m. when the cleaning crew had detected a strong odor of gunpowder outside his office and alerted the security police.

Julie could almost feel the apartment's quietness; there was not the usual hum of morning traffic. It was Saturday, she realized, and for a disoriented instant she enjoyed the thought of not having to go into the office. Wake up, Julie. It's nightmare time again.

★

A Forthcoming Worldwide Mystery by
DOROTHY SALISBURY DAVIS

THE HABIT OF FEAR

DOROTHY
SALISBURY DAVIS
LULLABY OF MURDER

W✪RLDWIDE®

TORONTO • NEW YORK • LONDON • PARIS
AMSTERDAM • STOCKHOLM • HAMBURG
ATHENS • MILAN • TOKYO • SYDNEY

LULLABY OF MURDER

A Worldwide Mystery/March 1989

This edition is reprinted by arrangement with Charles
Scribner's Sons, a division of Macmillan, Inc.

ISBN 0-373-26021-0

For
David Lieberman

ONE

JEFF SAMPLED HIS MARTINI—straight up, no rocks—and approved, which seemed to surprise him. He was even more meticulous about martinis than about most things. Outside the states he travelled with a little vial of vermouth in his inside pocket and always ordered straight gin. The drink judged worthy of the toast, he met Julie's eyes and proposed: "To your own by-line by this time next year."

Julie wrinkled her nose and murmured thanks. She turned her glass round and round, an orange blossom that, sooner or later, she would be expected to drink. Finally she lifted it: "To Paris and to you."

"In that order?"

She grinned. "I'm very fond of both of you."

The restaurant noises picked up as a party shuffled its seating arrangement. Someone was explaining that the guest of honor must face the door through which, at Sardi's, the rich and famous were presumably in constant transit.

Jeff scowled and sipped his drink. Sardi's was not his favorite restaurant, but it was Julie's the last time he'd asked and he insisted on it. The occasion was more noteworthy for her solid year of employment on the gossip column, *Tony Alexander Says...*, than for Jeff's departure later that night for Paris. Geoffrey Hayes' *Times* assignments took him to distant and troubled places, Julie's to where her legs could carry her, so to speak. She suspected he was already half way to Paris and envied him the depth of his work, its significance. "Where do you start when you get there?" she asked.

"I'll skirmish around a bit and try to improve my contacts. France is a conspirators' marketplace. I'll be shopping for discarded loyalties. How's that?"

"Very fancy," Julie said.

Jeff laughed aloud.

She conjured a picture of him sitting in a smoky bistro, drinking beer and waiting for someone who would walk past the place twice to get a look at him before going in. She had not questioned whether he would be in danger. Risk was to be taken for granted. So was caution. He was going to do a series on the neo-Fascist movement. "I'd like to be going with you," she said. "I'd like to work on something that important."

Jeff made a sound in his throat that suggested satisfaction with things as they were. He neither under- nor over-valued the job of legman for Tony Alexander. It was where he too had started his newspaper career.

She laid her hand on his across the table. The grey in his hair was becoming dominant and made him even more distinguished-looking. The probing dark eyes suggested a worldly wisdom, the firm mouth, self-assurance almost to a degree of self-satisfaction.

"You should work on your French," Jeff said. "We could speak it at home, couldn't we? Good for both of us."

She felt slightly irritated, no doubt because she was self-conscious about her French. His was always going to be so much better. She was on the point of suggesting that it might improve their communication and then held back. They did not communicate well when they were together too much. Their marriage thrived on honeymoons and separations.

He squeezed her hand and released it. "Why do you always look your most enchanting when I'm on my way to the airport?"

She bit back the answer to that one too. "Rhetorical question, right?" But she knew that she took more patience with her makeup and dressed better when he was home. With the job she would keep it up to some extent, but part of her longed to revert to jeans and sneakers and something with pockets. Then almost at once she preferred her present chicness. Maybe the gamin in her was forever banished, and no one would miss it more than Jeff...his little girl, his elf. Let her go. God bless her, but let her go.

"I'm not your only admirer," Jeff added. "There's an old boy at a wall table who can't take his eyes off you."

"Always the old boys," Julie said and shifted her position so that she could discreetly glance in the direction Jeff had indicated. "That's Jay Phillips, the press agent. He was one of the first people Tony sent me to and he's been great to me ever since."

"In my day we steered clear of publicity handouts," Jeff said and took up the wine list. "Tonight you'll have wine." He always said it and she always did have wine nowadays. She even enjoyed it, but Jeff had missed the transition. "A roughish Burgundy," he mumbled to himself. He settled for a Pommard, trusting the importer, a name he knew better than he knew the cellar of Sardi's. "Pommard is a chancy wine, but very good with duck if you get the right one."

"And the right duck," Julie said.

Jeff's second martini came with their shrimp. He looked at his watch: he was not in that much of a hurry.

"Eight o'clock curtain," Julie said in defense of the express service.

He ignored the shrimp for the time being and sipped his drink. "Do you like working for Tony, or are you proving something?"

"Both. I'm hanging in there and I like that. And I do like the job and I don't settle for handouts."

"Of course you don't," he soothed. "Don't misunderstand. I'm very proud of you."

"Thank you," she said, bristling underneath at the fatherliness. There were times she resented Tony for the same reason. The person whose parent-like advice she accepted was Fran, Tony's wife, who was about Jeff's age and a lot younger than Tony. She had not seen her for months. "Jeff, why don't we see the Alexanders socially anymore? Is it because I work for Tony?" She knew Jeff and Tony often met at the Press Club.

"Julie, it's not your fault."

"I didn't say it was." But she had a habit of taking blame whenever it was available. "I miss Fran. That's all."

"Then why don't you stop at the shop and see her?" Fran owned a flower shop on Lexington Avenue. "Or call her up and take her to lunch. She'd like that. She's always been very fond of you."

"Jeff, you're being—I don't know what exactly..."

"Pompous?"

"Patronizing."

"Am I?" he said distantly and pulled the shrimp to where he could spear one of them. "Your friend the press agent is headed this way. He's sloshed if I'm not mistaken."

"You're not," Julie said, not having to look and not unhappy at the diversion. She wondered if what she and Jeff were doing was not a kind of ritual that prepared them for separation. She'd been through it before: *distancing* was the word that came to mind.

Phillips came up to the table, a big man, his face chunky and flushed. He was well known as a Broadway publicist and as a heavy drinker. He stood a moment, almost steady, and finally arrived at what he wanted to say. "I just wanted to tell you, Mr. Hayes, how much I admire your wife." He enunciated each word carefully. "Can't read you, I admit, but I do admire your wife."

"That's good enough," Jeff said gallantly.

Julie thought of introducing them. It seemed superfluous.

"A real lady. They don't make many of them anymore." He put a hand on the table as though to steady it.

Julie could feel the color rise to her face. The diners nearby were looking at them. "Could I stop around later at the theater and see you?"

"No, my dear, you could not because I won't be there. My services to Dorfman Productions have been terminated."

"I'm sorry." He had lost, it would seem, three of the biggest shows in town.

The man looked blubbery as he stared down at her. He lifted heavy eyes and settled them on Jeff. "How does someone as nice as her work for an s.o.b. like Alexander? Do you understand it?"

Jeff touched his napkin to his lips. "I try."

Phillips shook hands with each of them and drew himself up very straight. He walked from the restaurant like a man on a tightrope.

"As I was going to tell you in any case," Jeff said, "Tony and I exchanged compliments today. I'm an elitist snob and I called him an illiterate parasite."

"I thought Tony was your best friend. I thought that's why I got a job with him."

"You got a job with him because you could do the work."

"Okay, but I don't think he knew that when he hired me. I didn't know it myself."

"I did," Jeff said.

Which brought them back to square one. Julie was on the edge of becoming irritable again and there wasn't time to work it out. "Jeff, is Tony really an s.o.b.?"

"It's you that's worked for him this past year," Jeff said, a little mockingly.

"But he's your friend, damn it. And you worked for him once yourself."

"I don't test my friends by their virtue. No more do you. Stop and think: Sweets Romano?" He referred to the gentlemanly, art-collecting gangster with whom Julie had twice shared a most unlikely partnership in ferreting out criminal mischief. Her acquaintanceship with Romano had gone a long way toward recommending her for *Tony Alexander Says....* Tony had expected a direct line to the underworld.

"Shall we call it a draw?" Julie said with a puckered smile that got to Jeff every time.

He nodded but both of them knew that the eleven o'clock flight was taking off for Paris just in time.

TWO

ON HER WAY TO WORK in the morning Julie figured out that Jeff would already have had his lunch. In the lobby of the *New York Daily* building the huge globe turned, the world on a sunken axis; a Japanese couple, the man with a camera and numerous attachments slung from straps around his neck, stood at the railing and beamed as Japan went by. On the back wall one of the clocks that told the times around the world showed it to be five minutes to three in Paris, September 15. In New York it was five minutes to ten of the same day. As usual, Jeff was way ahead of her.

Tony sat at his desk looking about as fresh as a ripe avocado. On early morning appearances he often looked as though he had not been to bed, and sometimes he hadn't. When Julie walked in he checked his watch and said to Tim Noble, the other of his apprentices, "I owe you a buck. She's early."

Alice Arthur, everybody's secretary, was clacking away, transcribing tapes. With Julie's arrival she took off the earphones and picked up her shorthand book.

Tony lumbered to his place at the head of the conference table. He had to be well into his sixties. His hair was white, his eyebrows black and ferocious, overhanging dark, bloodshot eyes. The white mustache was exotic though slightly tarnished at the tips from twistings. Jeff was right: it was ridiculous that she had worked with him for a year and couldn't say whether or not he was a bastard. She did have trouble with her father images.

Tony gazed at her morosely. "You're looking peaked this morning. Too much bon voyaging?"

"No."

"The eminent journalist did depart, didn't he?"

Julie nodded.

"In nebulae of self-importance?"

"Come off it, Tony."

"Tut, tut, tut. Only the truth will set you free."

He *was* a bastard.

Tony sat back and chortled as though he had read her mind. "Now. What have you got for me to sign off with for the week-end, either of you? I want something both frolicsome and wicked."

Tim brushed back a wisp of hair from his forehead and told of a presidential widow who was going to play the role of herself in a Broadway musical.

"Danse macabre," Tony said: "Write it up. And you, my peaked one, have something too?"

"I understand Jay Phillips has been fired from the Michael Dorfman shows."

"And do you know the reason?"

"I didn't ask, but I assume it's booze."

"*Assume.* What a fancy word for a leglady, and one too much of a lady to ask."

"I'm not all that much of a lady." Not what she meant to say at all, but her reputation for femininity was getting out of hand. "I'll find out from another source."

"I wouldn't bother," Tony said wearily.

Across the table Tim Noble asked earnestly: "Do press agents ever make news, boss?"

"Only when it's in very short supply." Tony swung round on Julie again. "All right, sweetheart: I've got a story for you. Let's see what you can do with it. There's a place called Garden of Roses on Amsterdam Avenue up near Harlem. In the days of the big bands it was a ballroom. It's being refurbished by a character who proposes to revive the dance marathon—a fad or a phenomenon, whatever you want to call it—of the nineteen-thirties."

"I wasn't even born then," Julie said.

"I was already a handsome beggar, if I say it myself. I won two hundred dollars in a dance marathon—and these damned varicose veins." He pushed away from the table and planted a foot on its edge. He pulled up the leg of his slacks.

Tim Noble half-rose and peered down at the hairy leg through which the swollen veins were just visible. He looked at Tony over his glasses. Tim had a pixie-like quality and could get away with almost anything with Tony. "Never saw anything like it, Sir. Can you make them ripple?"

Tony withdrew the leg. He glowered at Tim, then at Julie and smiled ominously. "Why don't the two of you go up there and sign on as contestants?"

"Please, Tony, I don't want varicose veins," Julie said.

"Okay, sweetheart. But do me something with feeling."

He got up and crossed the room to the video data terminal, settled himself comfortably before the screen, took a handful of notes from his pocket and began to tap out the next day's column.

Julie searched the movie listings in *The New Yorker* hoping that *They Shoot Horses, Don't They?* was playing somewhere. Tim had suggested it for background information on the dance marathon. No luck. She was about to phone the Reference Room of the Public Library when she thought of Mary Ryan, an older friend, who was great on the New York retrospective, the theater, and such events as the blackout, two World Fairs, Mayor LaGuardia reading the funny papers....

"Oh, I remember them well," Mrs. Ryan said of the dance marathons when Julie reached her. "I wasn't long in this country. And let me tell you, it wasn't milk and honey we came over to in those days. Respectable men were on the streets selling pencils and shoe-laces. I must have been in my second or third year of highschool and I remember, this chum and I thought it would be a great lark to stay out all night. Come over and have a cup of tea with me and I'll tell you about it. We wound up at a dance marathon, you see."

The trouble with going to Mrs. Ryan's was that you'd be asked on arrival to take Fritzie for a walk, and Fritzie was an elderly dachshund who took his time about everything. "Mrs. Ryan, let's meet at the shop, okay?"

"The shop" was a low-rental ground floor in a tenement building on West Forty-fourth Street, not far from the Willoughby where Mrs. Ryan lived. Julie still used it for an office. She had acquired it with Mrs. Ryan's prodding really. She had been on her way to buy a set of Tarot cards one day, largely for her own amusement, when she chanced to meet Mary Ryan with whom, until then, she'd had but a nodding acquaintance through their mutual interest in theater. It happened at a time when Julie felt rudderless—Jeff was away and her then therapist, Doctor Callahan, had said she couldn't help her until Julie was serious about helping herself. A job was strongly recommended. With almost childish pique, Julie took to the notion of setting up as a "reader and advisor," and Mary Ryan had cheered her on.

Julie had long since taken down her sign from the window, but she had hung onto the shop at Jeff's suggestion, a place of her own. Its location was highly symbolic of a side of her nature that she didn't understand herself, a fondness for people who worked at humble occupations. Dr. Callahan had called it a cop-out, a place where Julie had no relationship problems, where she didn't have to compete. Which was partly true, but not the whole story. The shop was less than a block from the Actors Forum, where she had once been an active member and still had many friends. There was always someone on the street to greet her as though she'd been there yesterday even when she hadn't been around for weeks. Mrs. Rodriguez, her upstairs neighbor, kept an almost constant look-out from her elbow cushion in the window. She had been invaded recently by her husband's relatives from San Juan. Julie felt guilty about not offering to sublet her place to them when they needed more room, but Rose Rodriguez didn't like the idea at all. "They pay me," she said and thumped her bosom righteously. "It makes up." What it made up for was the "trick" she could no longer entertain while her husband was working. Juanita, Rose's silent child, had finally gone to school. Now, when she played on the stoop, the dolls were neater and most of them had arms and legs and even hair. Julie figured out that Juanita was playing teacher instead of mother these days, and sometimes her two smaller cousins were allowed to attend school with the dolls. Juanita wasn't silent anymore either: she screamed at all of them, "Speak English!"

The kettle was boiling on the hotplate by the time Mrs. Ryan arrived. She looked a little more beery every time Julie saw her, the grey hair more straggly beneath the limp straw hat, the pale blue eyes more watery. She had been an usher at the Martin Beck most of her working life and though long retired she still lived a stone's throw from the theater. "What I like about you, Julie," she said when she had looked over the shop to see if there was anything new, which there wasn't, "is the way you never forget your friends."

Julie addressed herself to the dog. She got a biscuit from the tin box on top of the dresser. Fritzie was already sitting up, supporting himself with one paw on the dresser; his stomach sagged obscenely. "You're putting on a little weight, old boy."

"He's fading away to a ton," Mrs. Ryan said, and settled into one of the four director's chairs that surrounded the cut-down table. A large crystal ball was the table's only ornament.

Julie served the tea double strength and blisteringly hot. Mary Ryan paid her a compliment she had heard more than once. "You've a drop of Irish blood in you somewhere to make tea like that." When the old woman had emptied the cup to the last few drops, she turned it round and round to shape a fortune for herself in the leaves. She put the cup aside, however, without a word on what she saw. "Now I did tell you my chum and I went to the movies," she said, groping her way into the past.

"It wasn't even midnight when we got out of the last show. I forget what we saw.... Did I say that we told her parents we were at my house and told mine that we were at hers? They'd have gone out of their minds if they'd known. We went to a Chinese restaurant on Broadway, one of those places you went upstairs and you couldn't get the smell of the incense out of your clothes for days..."

Julie gave Fritzie a lift onto the chair he'd been trying to get aboard.

"I don't suppose you need all these details," Mrs. Ryan said, hoping to be contradicted.

"It's mostly the dance marathon," Julie admitted. "Whatever you can remember about that."

"What I remember most about it was the way the poor creatures would hang on one another, dying for sleep, and all of a sudden the orchestra would speed them up, playing something snappy like *Happy Days Are Here Again*. I'm ashamed to say it, but there I was in the front row clapping my hands off."

"Spectator sport," Julie said.

"Or maybe I was trying to keep myself awake. It was the longest night of my life and as I look back on it now, a wake would have been more fun. If only we'd had the sense to look for a nice Irish wake..." Mrs. Ryan's voice faded and her eyes misted with some memory she did not share. Then: "Isn't it a shame about Jay Phillips? Do you know him? But of course you would in the job you have now."

"What about him?"

"He committed suicide last night. I heard it on the radio just as I was leaving the house. He jumped from the George Washington Bridge, but they didn't find his body until after daylight. It was all the way down near Ninety-sixth Street."

THREE

JULIE TOOK the graffiti-spattered Broadway train uptown. When she had used to travel to and from Miss Page's School by public transportation she had felt a comradeship with the other riders. She often made up lives for them between stops. Now people huddled inside themselves as though an outward glance might commit them to something. She kept thinking of Jay Phillips. He'd been putting things in order, in his fuddled way, sitting in Sardi's Restaurant. She and Jeff had simply fallen within his line of vision and become a brief distraction. She'd left Mrs. Ryan speculating on whether there would be a wake. The old church, she explained, would have denied him Christian burial, a suicide, despair being the ultimate sin. The new church made allowances for most things that weren't sexual.

What had Tony done, she wondered, to have turned the man against him. Something recent—or something past but not forgiven? She'd always thought of Phillips as a considerate person with a barely controlled drinking problem. The worst language she had ever heard him use was his reference to Tony as an s.o.b. Practically archaic.

The Garden of Roses was a huge, baroque edifice, the cornerstone of which had been laid in 1922. A cement bas-relief of roses overhung the entrance. New glass doors were going up where the carpenters tore away the boards. People formed a line outside, to apply for employment, Julie supposed. There were a table and a few folding chairs in the lobby. A haze of dust made the harsh work lights within the building softer. She inquired where the office was, and then the name of the person in charge.

"I guarantee you'll never forget it, Miss: Mr. Morton Butts."

She found Mr. Butts behind a cluttered desk. On top of the clutter were what looked like two sets of blueprints held open by a hammer and a pair of pliers, a Pepsi bottle and a bible. He slipped one of the prints over the other and let them roll up together as Julie approached. He introduced himself and dusted a chair for her with his breast pocket handkerchief.

"Why a dance marathon?" he repeated her first question and took off. "What you got to understand about me, Miss, I'm a student of history. That way when something everybody else thinks is new comes along I know when and where it showed up the last time and what made it click then. If it didn't click it didn't make history. See what I mean?"

Julie nodded.

"And there's always room for improvement. But you got to do everything with heart. You got to believe in it. And in yourself." He thumped his chest with a chubby fist. "I've been working almost a year on this project, and two weeks from now the lights go on. Let me tell you how it works. Ten thousand dollars at the top, winner take all. No second, third, no consolation prize: it's do or die." Mr. Butts' face was ruddy and his thick short greying hair stood up on his head like a scrub brush. Round and plump, he was very little taller than Julie. He had to be about sixty or so. His eyes, with the glint of a zealot in them, were as busy as lightning bugs, and the spittle flew from his mouth with his enthusiasm. Every now and then he would get up from the desk and go to the window, taking the blueprints with him, tapping them in the palm of his hand as he stood on tiptoe to see the lineup below. They were would-be contestants, he explained, who were paying twenty dollars a head for the privilege. Their registration fee would also buy them a good physical examination.

"There's something about the dance marathon you wouldn't understand if you didn't know your history: it was one of the important ways the American people pulled themselves out of the Great Depression in the nineteen-thirties. Most of the schoolbooks teach you it was Franklin D. Roosevelt that saved the country with his alphabet soup,

the AAA and the WPA, and the NRA.... Don't you believe it. What saved this country was the people with their
natural grit and determination to do things for themselves.
The dance marathon was a test of that grit."

"My boss got varicose veins from the one he was in,"
Julie said.

"And he's proud of them now, isn't he?"

"I guess so," Julie said, "or I wouldn't be here."

Mr. Butts tucked the blueprints into an already stuffed
desk drawer and bounced toward the door. "Let me show
you through the plant. We have a few days' work to do yet,
but you'll get the idea."

He smelled of soap, the scouring kind, or else something
he used to try to flatten his hair. Taking Julie by the arm, he
propelled her into what had been the main ballroom; good
hardwood floors, as he pointed out. You couldn't buy lumber like that anymore even if you could afford it. Workmen
were putting up railings, creating what looked like a minia-
ture race course. "We'll gradually bring down the number
of times per day a couple has to circle the track to stay in
competition, but the winners have got to make at least one
entire go-round the day the dance ends."

"And if they can't?" Julie asked, remembering Mrs.
Ryan's description of "the poor creatures."

"No such word, Mrs. Hayes. If they *don't*, the prize
doubles in a new contest."

"I see," she murmured.

He took her arm again and steered her from one to another of the rooms at one end of the dance floor: shower
rooms and toilets, a room for cots, an infirmary where a
doctor would be on duty twenty-four hours a day—an un-
derpaid resident from the nearest hospital, Julie suspected—a snack bar. The contestants would have ten
minutes out of every hour to attend to their personal business. He showed her where the sponsors' boxes would be
built and where he would be putting in a bank of seats for
the audience. One area was designated "media." The Garden of Roses had been built to accommodate thousands.

"Live music?" Julie asked.

"Three nights a week and Sunday afternoons. Otherwise..." He let go of her arm and rollicked along the railing to a platform where there might once have been an organ console. Now it was an electronic switchboard. He chose from among the rows of buttons and threw a switch. The whole room exploded with rock music. He doused the work lights and pulled another switch: strobe lights streaked across the backs and faces of the men who had been working until the lights went out. The illusion of grimacing faces, disjointed body motions and the hard, loud music: an interlude of madness in what didn't seem like a very sane operation altogether. Butts switched things back to normal and trotted back to Julie. "Now, what else can I show you?"

Show, not tell, Julie observed. Quibbling, but for all his volubility, he was talking for the purpose of avoiding questions rather than answering them. "How come the Garden of Roses?" Julie asked.

"It was here. As simple as that, and rather than let it deteriorate I persuaded the city to lease it to me for five years. There has been talk of its demolition. Talk also of its possible landmark status. I look upon my enterprise as a holding action."

"Tell me something about you," Julie said. "Have you always been in show business?"

"You might say so. I view life as a showcase and God as producer. I've been with the circus, I've been real deep in religion. I've promoted boxing matches and built gymnasiums to teach the manly art of self defense. But, getting down to the nitty-gritty, I'm just an old-fashioned businessman, American to the core, and it won't hurt these days to put that in your interview."

"Got it," Julie said. "I'd like to talk to a few of the contestants, if you don't mind."

"Why should I mind? I expect the mayor to show up for the grand opening so you know everything's got to be kosher. Only remember, they're not contestants until they've passed their physicals."

He walked her back to the lobby. The line of registrants was growing, mostly blacks and Hispanics. "A real Amer-

ican mix," he said and smiled happily. Tiny, sharp teeth, but
his own. He gave her a moist marshmallow of a hand to
shake and added, "Come to the opening and bring the boss
with you."

UNEMPLOYED DISHWASHERS, cabdrivers, city layoffs,
waitresses, beauticians, hospital workers: they expected to
be on television, marathon dancers, and considered Julie
their opening round of publicity. Everybody claimed to have
heard of Tony Alexander, and by the time Julie moved down
the line, they had.

   She crossed the street and looked back. Most of them
waved. Was the building rococo or baroque? She tended to
mix the two. It might not matter to the readers of *Tony Alexander Says*...but it had better matter to the wife of
Geoffrey Hayes. She proposed to look it up in the *Architectural Guide to New York City* when she got back to the
office. The "Garden" looked as though it would take a
fortune to restore. It looked as though it would take a fortune even to demolish. In the distance were vast complexes
of public housing, brick, glass and mortar, and if you
looked at them in a certain way you could imagine them on
a slow march downtown. How many buildings similar to
this monstrous citadel of dance had made way? On the other
hand, Columbia University at her back seemed eternal. Not
far away was St. Luke's Hospital, and beyond, the massive
Cathedral of St. John the Divine. Yet Amsterdam Avenue,
as it headed up toward 125th Street, was a parade of small,
neighborhood shops, appealing to what Butts had called "a
real American mix."

   There was something incongruous about the whole project, she felt. Or was it the idea of a dance marathon itself?
How had it come to Tony's attention, she wondered. Certainly it had piqued his interest. The building was out of
sync with the present neighborhood, too large, too gaudy;
why had it survived till now? And a five year lease? She
thought of the two sets of blueprints Butts had gathered up
and kept with him while she was there. Why hadn't he said,
"Here, look what we're doing," and *then* shown her the

actual scene? The property would have fallen to the city for delinquent taxes, she supposed. Was there something in the blueprints, a legend perhaps, that he had not wanted her to see?

Walking back to Broadway through the Columbia campus, she thought of calling the city public relations office to find out where to seek further information. She envisioned an afternoon of phone calls and days of waiting . . . only to discover that the Garden sat on a molehill. It occurred to her that she had a source uniquely her own. Sweets Romano reportedly owned more West Side real estate, under a variety of covers, than anyone. She found a pay phone in one of the library buildings and dialed his private number.

The routine was the same as always: she gave the number from which she was calling to the person answering, and within a couple of minutes the phone rang in the booth. "This is Romano. How pleasant to hear your voice, Miss Julie."

"As usual, I want something," Julie said.

"Anything within my power."

"This time it's information: a ballroom built in the 1920s called Garden of Roses on Amsterdam Avenue. It's being reopened and polished up for a dance marathon by a man named Butts. He's leased the building from the city."

"I know the building," Romano said.

"Is there anything strange about its survival till now? I don't really know what I'm looking for, Mr. Romano. The whole enterprise seems crazy to me. I mean what if it fails? All that money. . . . There's got to be more to the operation than putting on a few weeks of nostalgia. Maybe I'm wrong about him, but the entrepreneur seems to me a phoney."

"You've become a muckraker, Miss Julie?" It was half question, half teasing. She could imagine the cherubic face, ageless, utterly enigmatic. To her. And better that way. If she believed half the things told of him she'd be too scared to approach him at all.

"I wasn't sent up here to rake muck, but I have a feeling there's some of it around."

"And Mr. Alexander does cherish an occasional splash of investigative reportage—to clear his palate, as it were."

"Mmmm." What else could she say?

"Give me an hour," Romano said, and the phone clicked off.

Julie bought a *Post* and caught a bus that would put her down outside the *Daily* building. The page three story of Jay's death had the usual *Post* fillip: a picture of the bagged body being loaded into the mortuary vehicle. The heading read: *Theater Publicist Dies in Hudson Plunge*.

Shortly after midnight, popular Broadway publicist J. P. Phillips walked halfway across the George Washington Bridge intent on suicide. He succeeded. A motorist with a CB transmitter in his car saw him hurtle over the railing and alerted the police. The Coast Guard was on the scene within minutes, but it was not until dawn that the body was recovered several miles downstream.

Reached late this morning, Michael Dorfman, producer of three shows on which Phillips was currently working, said he could not imagine why the publicist would take his own life.

"Jay was one of the best-liked men in show business," Dorfman said. "I am shocked and saddened. Why would he do a thing like this?"

Phillips started his professional career as an actor and stage manager. He switched to publicity when he returned from World War II. He is survived by two sisters, Eileen and Mary Jean Phillips. His wife, the former Ellen Duprey, died several years ago.

Shocked and saddened. Nothing to suggest Dorfman had just fired the man. And she would probably never find out now why Jay Phillips felt as he had about Tony.

Alice Arthur was the only one in the office when Julie got back. She was typing and filling cards for Tony's "Celebrity bank." The drawers resembled the card file in any public library. The information was privileged bits on people in the news. The file would have been too hot to store on the newspaper premises, but Tony rented his own office in the *Daily* building several floors above the editorial offices.

Julie looked up the Garden of Roses. It was rococo, and a solitary example in the neighborhood, which ran to classic and gothic. She was well acquainted with the whole area by the time Alice filed her last card, covered her typewriter, disconnected the VDT and went home for the day. Julie called Romano again.

"Fascinating story, Miss Julie. I'm grateful to you for calling it to my attention. I collect political foibles. They tend to become useful in time. This potentially valuable property has been a political plaything for years. It went through a series of tax problems ending in forfeiture which you may detail for yourself from the public records. As for what I am about to say, I needn't remind you, your source is sacred."

"Absolutely sacred," Julie said.

"Just so: the most recent private owner seems to have persuaded the Transport Authority that it could be converted into a bus garage. Money was appropriated for one set of plans after another until a certain go-getter in the Council went up there with a plumb line and a pocket calculator and demonstrated the total impracticality of such conversion. The Garden of Roses languished. The building was condemned last year and the university contemplated purchase of the site. Suddenly it was unavailable. The present occupant leased it from the city for five years—I suspect for a pittance. I suppose it can be argued that during that time much of that area will go to public or privately funded housing, which in turn will determine the value of the real estate under that monstrous building. In any case, the gentleman with the curious name of Morton Butts has the lease on the property and has bought the condemned building for a token five hundred dollars. There you have it, Miss Julie, in its broadest outline."

"Five hundred dollars! There's five thousand dollars' worth of hardwood floors in the place."

"And not a trace of a bus skid on them. The operative word, Miss Julie, is condemned. To some, if I may be irreverent, it can mean salvation. Mind now, there is nothing truly sinister that I detect, but then if there were it wouldn't surface in an inquiry as limited as mine. And let me hasten to add, I should not wish to go further with it myself. My motives are always suspect, and whatever's afoot might go awry."

"I understand," Julie said, which she didn't. She knew Romano's wealth, his underworld reputation; she knew he was called "the king of porn," films of that ilk having once intrigued him; but she also knew that he had not left his penthouse home for years, that his art collection was famous, his manners impeccable, and his person—to her—a total mystery. He was chortling at his own turn of phrase.

"I'm very grateful to you, as usual," Julie said.

"Any time. Come to lunch soon, Miss Julie." And he was gone, his abruptness on the phone always putting her in mind of a magician's vanishing act.

JULIE BEGAN THE STORY "I never promised you a Rose Garden, only a ten thousand dollar prize," and wrote it to Butts' own style. He simply begged to be written as he spoke. She devoted a brief final paragraph to the property, all questions—which were more effective than answers—so if Tony chose, he could simply drop it off. She concluded, "Might it not have become a city garage or a learning site? But the Garden of Roses rises again as it fell, a gaudy citadel of dance."

Tim Noble checked in to drop his "items" in the copy box. He offered Julie tickets to an off off Broadway opening in the Bowery. She declined and gave one more polish to her piece and felt that it was good. She slipped it through the slot of the box on Tony's desk. You could put things in but you couldn't get them out without the key that Tony carried on a ring at his belt. Somebody, probably Tim, had pasted a legend above the slot: *Abandon hope, all ye who enter here.*

When she got home, all the messages with the telephone answering service were for Jeff, save one from Mary Ryan. Julie phoned her and learned that the friends of Jay Phillips were invited to call at the Murray Funeral Home on Second Avenue the following evening and that there would be a Mass at noon on Saturday.

"I'm thinking of going over to Murray's," Mrs. Ryan said. "He was always good to me—five dollars every Saturday night when he had a show in the house where I worked. Would you like to go along?"

"Well, yes," Julie said. "I would."

"There's a lovely pub next door called The Galway Bay. Maybe we could have a bite together first."

"I'll buy you dinner," Julie said.

"On the expense account?"

"Why not?" Julie said, although there was one good reason why not: she didn't have an expense account.

She answered those of Jeff's calls that required answers and declined two dinner invitations that, in politeness, were extended to her even in his absence. She then cleaned house and drew the living room drapes. She was unlikely to entertain in Jeff's absence, and she'd been getting pretty good at it, so long as he did the cooking. He seemed to have been away a lot longer than twenty-four hours.

FOUR

SHE GAVE the morning *Times* a quick scan. Jeff's column, still bearing a New York dateline, was headed *Industrial Reprisal*. She felt guilty about not reading it and thought again of her former therapist, a very direct woman: "Why can't you simply say the subject doesn't interest you?" Well, doctor...

The *Times* obituary on Phillips was clear and informative. It gave the plays and the theaters with which he had been associated, including summer stock, a species of legitimate theater almost extinct in the time Julie had made her try as an actress. She tore out the obit and put it in her carry-all.

She had not expected Tony to be in the office that early but he was, and from his smile she knew that something was wrong, probably with her story on Morton Butts. He had the copy in hand. With it he waved her into the chair in front of him.

"May I put my things away first, Tony?" Her carry-all.

"No."

She sat. Alice's typewriter had the rat-tat-tat of a machine gun. Tim started to leave the office like a stealthy cat. It ought to have been funny but it wasn't. Tony ordered him back to his desk and then silenced Alice and read aloud, "'I never promised you a Rose Garden...' How's that for originality?" He continued to read, his tone mockingly folksie. The copy sounded awful. He stopped abruptly before the last paragraph and addressed himself to Tim Noble. "Don't you think the gal ought to be working for *The New Yorker*?"

Tim was studying his fingernails. He didn't look up.

"Please, Tony, cut it out," Julie said.

"You don't know me very well, sweetheart. I sent you up there for a couple of paragraphs of nostalgia about the dance marathon and you turn me in a tight-assed homily. I ask for feeling and you give me style. Style stinks!" He threw down the single page of copy. "It's got no guts."

Julie would have given a lot to find out what was underneath the tirade. "I think there's feeling in it," she said and then plunged ahead although she knew it was a mistake: "I cared about those people lined up with twenty bucks in their hands and the dream of making it to television."

"God's truth, gal: you really cared?"

Julie bit her lip. She wasn't going to be able to stand up to him and she knew it.

"God's truth, do you remember a face among them? One face?"

She sat mute, determined not to cry.

"Blacks, Hispanics, poor whites, the bloody masses. Christ! I thought for a while you were a modern woman. Look, sweetheart, any one of them who got his twenty bucks up for a dream can get it up for bread if his hunger's in his belly. Sure, the dream is tawdry, but it's his dream, and he's going to read about it in Tony Alexander's column. And he's going to like what he reads."

Julie nodded. He'd made his point and she could see it.

But he wasn't letting up. "This Morton Butts character is right. I am proud of my varicose veins. I came to New York with one pair of shoes and a Woodstock typewriter. It was ten years before anyone knew I could write my name, much less a sentence."

"Okay, Tony. It's lousy. Let me try it again. What about that last paragraph? Does it interest you?"

"Not much. I take it you know the answers or you wouldn't ask the questions."

"I'd have to verify them from the public records," Julie said.

Tony smiled. Falsely. "What a lucky girl you are to have access to private records. What ever made you think of tapping such a source?"

It had occurred to her more than once that Tony both resented and coveted her Romano connection; there was no doubt in her mind now that he had correctly surmised of whom she'd asked her questions.

"It was just that Mr. Butts seemed like such a phony."

Tony didn't say a word. He sat staring at her, letting his eyes do the talking.

Julie's ego went down to floor level. "You may not want it for the column," she said pitifully, "but it's part of the Butts story all the same."

"I don't want it and I call the signals on this team."

"I got the message," Julie said, and getting to her feet, reached for the copy where it lay on the desk between them.

Tony thumped his hand down on it. "I said to drop it."

"The whole story?"

"The whole story."

"Okay, boss," she said and walked out of the office. She wasn't sure where she was going, but she needed to get away. What she wanted was to have another look at the copy herself. Tony had been using her stuff almost verbatim and she didn't think there was that much difference between today's copy and yesterday's.

Tim Noble caught up with her at the elevators. "Come on, I'll buy you coffee."

"I don't want coffee."

"All right. Orange juice."

"Tim, I think I'm going to quit."

Tim shrugged. "Sooner or later. It generally happens after he's stopped playing around with whomsoever."

"No kidding. You mean he blows up a storm with someone... after?"

"Never needed a pension plan for a gal yet. Except for Alice. No passes there."

"He's never made a pass at me either."

"He may be a bastard, but he's not a skunk."

"His friend's wife." But Julie had the feeling that what had kept her out of Tony's reach was that he didn't want to reach. She remembered sitting in a taxi with him once, holding hands. Long ago, before she'd asked him for a job.

She had been in such awe of him. God the Father. "Tell me straight, Tim, absolutely straight because I've got to know..."

He anticipated what she was going to say. "It isn't bad," he reassured her on the marathon piece.

"Would you tell me if it were?"

"It would depend."

The elevator dropped them to the ground floor without an intermediary stop. It seemed symbolic. Nothing was accidental, according to the Tarot. She was inclined to agree. "Tim, will he run anything on Jay Phillips?"

Tim gave a dry laugh. "I asked him that this morning and he says, 'You want to write obituaries? Write obituaries.'"

Julie paused at the railing surrounding planet earth. It orbited gently. "Am I crazy or is Tony on a bad trip?"

"Something."

She was tempted to tell him what Jay Phillips had said to her and Jeff at Sardi's. But why lay that on Tim, besides giving herself a shabby departure if she did quit? And somehow she wanted to quit, wanted more space, deeper waters. She was in a frame of mind that was going to require examination. It could be that she wasn't facing up. "Tim, it's great of you to offer me coffee, but I want to go home and think this out."

"Look. If you want to quit, don't. Make him fire you. Unemployment insurance, you know?" Which, though not in so many words, told Julie how tenuous a hold Tim thought she had on the job.

She managed a smile and stuck out her hand. "Thanks, Tim, for everything. I wouldn't have made it this far without you."

He hung onto her hand, shaking it thoroughly. He was such an odd-looking young man—big ears, a pointed chin— he looked like Fred Astaire in his Ginger Rogers days. "Julie, you've got no idea how many times I wanted to make a pass at you."

She threw her arms around him for one big hug and then got away quickly.

FIVE

JULIE HEADED FOR the shop, not home. The shop could use a good clean-up and she wanted madly to clean up something, to assuage the galloping anxiety. It was the thought of telling Jeff that gave her the most trouble, the humiliation, the helplessness, the old dependency. His little girl again—in whom he had confidence. Like hell. It was easy to say in retrospect. She probably ought to go the unemployment insurance route. From the cradle to the grave. She'd be on welfare if it weren't for Jeff. She could not think of a single person she wanted to see. Fritzie the dog maybe. But not Mrs. Ryan. Doctor Callahan. She ought to call the doctor and get a booster shot that would keep her on the job: gainful employment was a tenet of the therapist's religion. She thought of the priest at St. Malachy's who had told her to come and see him any time. Father Doyle's best thing was prostitutes. And old ladies who kept telling him the same sins over and over. Pride and penitence.

She pounded along Forty-second Street as far as Broadway: "Haughty, naughty Forty-second Street." Another hunk of nostalgia. In song and dance. No pimps or pushers in this version, everybody was for everybody, especially for the understudy who was going to make it big in the *Lullaby of Broadway* number. A flashy young black who smelled of marijuana sidled up to her where she waited at the curb for a change in traffic lights. "Fifty bucks, doll. I got the best on the street."

"Blow away," Julie said.

"That's my song, baby."

She changed directions, uptown, and crossed at Forty-fourth Street, shaking off the pusher. The lullaby of Broadway, yeah.

The trouble with the shop was that there wasn't much to clean unless you could start with a bulldozer. The vacuum-cleaner kept hiccoughing on bits of plaster. The walls weren't safe even for climbing. She settled presently with a cup of tea and her notebook, which was a fat record of non sequiturs, part story ideas, part journal, part character speculations on a lot of odd types. She went through the book for past appraisals of Tony Alexander. There was a time when she had liked him, his messy vests, his smelly pipe, but she had always been a little afraid of him, and much fonder of Fran, his wife. Jeff had said they were having trouble. Maybe that was Tony's whole problem, but she doubted it. There was a daughter whom Fran visited. Where? At school? Julie could not remember hearing of Tony's visiting her. Nor did he talk about her. Julie didn't even know her name. For a moment she wondered if the daughter was an invention, if Fran might have a life away from home covered by the daughter story. But who needed a cover story nowadays for anything? She thought about going to see Fran at the flower shop as Jeff had suggested; but if she did that now and word of it got to Tony.... Her pride couldn't take it.

By mid-afternoon she had decided to take Tim Noble's advice and hang in. Her history of hanging in was brief, her record of unemployment impressive. So, it was hustling time. She locked up the shop and walked over to the Actors Forum, where over the past year she had picked up a few items which Tony ran although he would never mention the Forum. He was not invited to their productions. It did no good to tell him that nobody from the press was invited. "Exactly," he would say. "That's what's wrong with the place. No accountability." It never occurred to him to wonder why an actors' workshop should be accountable to a gossip columnist.

Most of the actors sitting around the green room that afternoon waiting for rehearsal space, or just waiting, were young and only a few knew who Jay Phillips was when Julie asked if any of them had ever worked with him. Somebody recalled one thing about him: he couldn't stand backstage mothers.

"Who can? They're always pushing," Reggie Bauer said. "I almost made it as a child star and my own mother shot me down. She demanded they put me in Liza Minnelli's dressing room."

"With or without Miss Minnelli?"

Madge Higgens hung up the phone mid-dial and hooked her coin out of the return box. "Something you just said reminded me of something. Now I forget what." She came and sat on the arm of the sofa alongside Julie.

"About Jay?"

Madge nodded. She was a good actress and she'd been on the scene a lot longer than most of those present.

"Or about Liza and me?" Reggie prompted.

"Oh, shut up, Reggie.... When I was in *Autumn Tears*—it must be ten years ago—Jay was our press agent. Something unpleasant happened during the run and I can't get hold of it now. Isn't that ridiculous? I suppose I'd remember if it concerned me."

"Did you play the lead?" Julie asked. She had no recollection at all of *Autumn Tears*.

"No, and it had a child star, Patti Royce. Funny, nobody's ever heard of her in years and suddenly she's in a soap opera. Anyway, it was about a youngster disabled in an accident out to get revenge on the driver of the car. I played her mother. It wasn't a great play."

"The premise is false," a young woman whose name Julie didn't know said didactically. "I have never known a disabled person who wasn't upbeat."

"*Whose Life Is It Anyway?*" Reggie cited.

"That's up!" half the group shouted.

It was some minutes before Julie could get Madge back to *Autumn Tears*. "Patti Royce's mother would have been backstage, right?"

"And I don't remember her. I might as well make my phone call." Over her shoulder she said, "Can a person become senile before they turn forty?"

"It depends on how long it takes you to turn forty," Reggie said.

Having made the appropriate response to that, Madge put in her dime and dialed. Then she cried out: "I've got it! It has nothing to do with the play. Jay's wife died during the run, and if I'm not mistaken, she committed suicide."

JULIE WENT to the Newspaper Library, which wasn't far from the Forum. *Autumn Tears* was noted by two entries in the *New York Times Index*, its opening and its closing. It had run three weeks; the producer was Michael Dorfman. The *Times* review was terrible... "Patti Royce can't make up her mind whether she wants to be Marilyn Monroe or Judith Anderson when she grows up..." She looked up the name Phillips in the same year. There were more Phillipses than she would have thought. She found a brief story on the obituary page:

The actress Ellen Duprey Phillips died yesterday in a leap or fall from the roof of the Hotel Canada on East 58th Street. Mrs. Phillips, wife of the publicist J. P. Phillips, had been in ill health for some time.

Julie looked up the story in the other newspapers. The variation was only in additional credits to what had been at best a thin theatrical career. She sat a moment thinking of the next source, staring out at the heavily overcast sky. It was a bleak, chilly day and she felt as though she was getting a cold. What was her purpose in this research? To work up something Tony wouldn't run anyway? Trying to provoke him further?

No. It was the feeling of an unfinished story that pressed upon her. The incidence of the two suicides added a certain poignancy. She tried another tack and got out two weeks of microfilm copies of the *New York Daily* from the date of Mrs. Phillips' death forward. She read seven *Tony Alexander Says...* columns before coming on this item:

SMALL SAD WORLD: the hotel from which Ellen
Duprey Phillips leaped eighteen stories to her death is
the residence of Patti Royce, the child star of *Autumn
Tears*. Mrs. Phillips' widower, Jay, is publicity rep for
the play.

Small sad world. Julie jotted down the words, the source
and the date in her notebook; too many times she had had
to double back in her research for something she had
thought she would never need again. She wanted to know
now what Mrs. Phillips was doing in the Hotel Canada, and
if or how her presence there connected with Patti Royce, and
if that connection was what Tony was hinting at in the column. She also wanted to know where it fell in the chronol-
ogy of Jay's dislike for Tony.

She went back to the shop and called Celebrity Service for
the name of Patti Royce's agent. She then called Ted
Macken at Creative Talent, Inc. and asked if he would set
up an interview for her with Patti Royce. She identified
herself only as with the *New York Daily* and gave her shop
number. He promised to get back to her before five.

As she thought about it during the afternoon, Julie felt
she had a good angle for a column item in Patti Royce: not
the Phillips business—that would be something she might
query in passing—but in the story of a child star who had
fallen out of sight and was trying to make it back ten years
later in daytime television.

When the agent hadn't called back by five o'clock, Julie
phoned again. He was in conference. She left her number
again. At half-past five she tried again to reach him; he had
left the office for the day. No message. What in hell did he
think? That she was still an unemployed actress?

SIX

THE GALWAY BAY Bar and Grill, on Second Avenue in the
Eighties, was named after a horse, Julie discovered, not the
inside of an Irish peninsula. There was a male, gaslight at-
mosphere to the place, dark wood, brass fixtures, walls
teeming with photographs and prints of horses and riders,
the hunt, and slobbery-looking hound dogs. The smells were
of damp wool, beer and tobacco, and among the clamor of
voices, a soprano note rarely sounded. Mrs. Ryan had
phoned for a reservation in Julie's name, and when it was
called she nudged Julie forward.

The older woman settled herself opposite Julie in the
booth and gave her shoulders a rolling shrug like a pigeon
in out of the rain. "As you notice," she said, "I got out my
fall hat."

"Beautiful," Julie murmured.

"It's not beautiful at all, but it's what I have." She removed the hat. "You'd better have a whiskey if you're getting the sniffles."

"I don't know what I'm getting," Julie said. She ordered a vodka and orange juice on the side. No orange juice
at the Galway Bay. Tonic.

Mrs. Ryan ordered a bottle of lager. And a whiskey on the
side. "As a precaution, dear."

She laughed politely at Julie's account of the Butts interview. Which suggested that it was not as amusing as Julie
had thought. "And you know," Mrs. Ryan said, "people
did feel different in those days. Nobody *wanted* to be on the
WPA.... What an odd name, Butts. And yet I have a feeling it's Irish."

"Tony wasn't amused at all. I could lose my job over
what I wrote. Or over something."

Mrs. Ryan made a noise that didn't sound much like sympathy. Then: "You know, women were laid off in those days to make more jobs for the men." If Julie lost her job it wasn't going to be a major tragedy: she had Geoffrey Hayes to support her.

During the service of their dinner—by a waiter with starched cuffs shooting out from the sleeves of his shiny black jacket—Julie mused on what it would be like to be simply Mrs. Geoffrey Hayes and sit on the boards of certain charities, arrange theater benefits, and have other ladies in to tea so that the living room would be kept in operation even while Jeff was away.

"Lamb chops are such a luxury," Mrs. Ryan said.

Julie agreed but didn't say so.

"Julie, did you tell me that Mr. Phillips had lost his theater accounts?"

"Did I?" That was what she thought Mrs. Ryan was talking about when she spoke of the terrible thing that had happened to him.

"I thought you did, but not a word of it has come out in the papers."

"I noticed," Julie said. "We shouldn't listen to rumors."

MRS. RYAN asked the immaculate young man at the reception desk of Murray's where Mr. Phillips was "laid out." He looked shocked and accompanied them to the elevator.

A priest was saying the rosary. Mrs. Ryan eased herself down among those on their knees and groped in her purse for her beads. Julie stood as did most of the mourners in a respectful silence. Knees were pretty much out in the modern church. The large room was not crowded: fifty or so people, including those in an alcove talking softly among themselves. Michael Dorfman was there. Two older women in black knelt near the priest alongside the casket. They would be Jay's two unmarried sisters: they looked as though they belonged in another country and another time. The casket was blanketed with red roses. The rich chant of the priest's voice repeating the prayers over and over turned

Julie's mind to her own vagrant father, supposedly an Irish diplomat. Whatever its source, depression swept in on her like a fog. *"In the name of the Father, the Son, and the Holy Spirit..."*

She helped Mrs. Ryan to her feet.

"I'll say a word to the family," Mrs. Ryan said.

Julie edged her way toward the ante-room where the producer, Dorfman, and a couple of other members of the theater hierarchy were biding time. He looked at Julie, not sure whether he knew her or not. A dark, stocky man in middle age with thinning hair and eyes that bulged, he acted nervy and played with a cigarette. No one else was smoking, but Julie spotted an ashtray and took it to him. "I'm Julie Hayes," she said.

"Ah, yes." The name didn't mean a thing to him.

"I think I was one of the last people to talk with Jay—just a few hours before he died."

"It's hard to believe, isn't it?" Dorfman murmured. He was still trying to place her.

"He told me you'd fired him from all your shows."

"Rubbish. The man was paranoid. It's a drinker's problem."

"Which never seemed to get in the way of his work."

"What's your point, Miss Hayes?"

"No point especially, except that I don't see why he'd tell me he was fired if it weren't so."

"Any reason for him to tell you, if it were so?"

"Ha!" a small laugh when she wanted to squirm. "One thing for sure, Mr. Dorfman, something had gone wrong for him."

"He was drinking, and it's true, I was getting to be the only man on the street who would hire him. Now I must go, if you'll excuse me..." He thrust the ashtray back into Julie's hands and pocketed the unlit cigarette.

Kate Wylie, a second-string reviewer for the *Daily* arrived and headed straight for him. She managed a quick "Hi" to Julie. Then: "Mr. Dorfman, I saw the run-through this afternoon. Trish Tompkins is going to be terrific, better even than Abby."

"I hope you're right. She went in tonight." He looked at his watch. "Can I give you a lift?"

Wylie, who had just arrived, departed, pausing however to sign the visitor's book before catching up with Dorfman. Julie got rid of the ashtray. She thought about who Abby could be, and then realized that of course, Abby Hill was playing the title role in *Little Dorrit*, the year's hit musical. Except that she wasn't if Trish Tompkins went in that night.

Mrs. Ryan was deep in conversation with the two ladies in black, all of them settled on gilded chairs. A cluster of older actors were reminiscing about the grand days of summer theater in some remote little town where you were the season's greatest attraction. Someone mentioned the Albion Playhouse where he'd worked with Jay as stage manager. The very mention of it sent them into laughter they were hard put to muffle. Dorfman looked round at them from where he waited for the elevator and said, "Hello, boys."

There was not much love in the looks they sent after him, those boys of seventy or so.

"This is my friend, Julie," Mrs. Ryan said when Julie approached the three women. "Miss Eileen Phillips and Miss Mary Jean Phillips." The sisters were even older than Mrs. Ryan and certainly older than Jay had been. Both were Irish plump, their faces made up as with a dusting of flour and with very little lipstick; their blue eyes were watery and bloodshot. Each gave Julie a gloved hand.

"I'm sorry about Jay," Julie said. "He was one of my favorite people."

"That's what everybody says—the most popular man on Broadway," Miss Eileen said. "Which of his plays were you in, dear?"

Julie smiled regretfully. "I'm in the same end of the business as Jay." She decided not to mention Tony Alexander to them.

But Mary Ryan volunteered: "She's an assistant to Tony Alexander, the *New York Daily* columnist. You know, *Tony Alexander Says . . .*?"

"Isn't that nice," Miss Mary Jean said, her lips tight against her teeth.

Even Mrs. Ryan felt the chill. "Julie, I'm having a Mass said for Jay from both of us." A soothing mix of religion and politics. "Are you wanting to go now?"

"I think I should."

"Then you go along yourself, dear. Jack Carroll lives at the Willoughby..." She nodded toward the reminiscing actors. "We can go down home together. It won't be the first time."

Julie touched the hands of the Phillips women and murmured, "I am sorry."

Mrs. Ryan got to her feet. "I'll walk out to the elevator with you." When they reached it she explained, "I wanted to tell you something out of their hearing. They were saying how their brother was always doing free publicity for this or that charity or for some friend who couldn't make it on his own. Did you know he was doing all the publicity for your dance marathon?"

"No," Julie said. "I didn't know that."

"Well, then. I've earned my supper, haven't I?"

JULIE BUTTONED her raincoat up to the throat and fastened the hood under her chin. It was raining harder than when they had come and a chilly wind had arisen. There were very few people on Second Avenue and it probably wasn't wise to walk, but she did it all the same, staying close to the curb. It was not the first time she had tried to walk herself out of trouble, even out of being sick which she considered a state of mind as much as of body. The shop windows behind their iron grilles put her in mind of a scene in the late, late show classic, *The Lost Weekend*, in which the alcoholic writer tries to pawn his typewriter on Yom Kippur. She found herself wondering if her father drank. Always, when her mood down-shifted, she thought about the father she had never known except in a handsome photograph. Dead or alive? She often wondered if she would ever know. And did nothing about trying to find out. The little she had of him might vanish altogether, the bit about his being an Irish diplomat.

She sometimes thought her mother had made that up: it would not be the first lie her mother had told her. Nor the last. The last was about how she was going away for a few weeks to get her health back. Instead she had died. Julie and Jeff had not been married long then. Julie had always thought her mother was in love with Jeff, until psychiatry taught her that the only real love in her life was Julie. She might have been able to cry tears of love instead of anger at her funeral if she had understood. Maybe not. It might have turned her off even more.

Her feet were soaking and she was down in the Forties when she admitted to herself where she wanted to go and that she was walking up her courage. She had the office keys in her purse and she wanted to look up several names in Tony's celebrity "bank"; Patti Royce, Abby Hill, Phillips—Jay and/or Ellen Duprey—and now especially Morton Butts.

On Forty-second Street her spirits lifted. The lights were brighter, the traffic heavier, and the glassy new hotels near the newspaper plant made that part of town seem its taxi center. What a contrast to Forty-second Street west. Her shoes squished and squeaked on the marble floor as she crossed the lobby to sign the night registry. She had marked down the hour, nine fifty, when her eye caught Tony's heavy scrawl near the top of the page. He had signed in at eight forty and was still up there unless he had skipped signing out. She had no intention of finding out.

She took a cab home and, honoring a long-standing promise to Jeff, asked the driver to wait until she got inside the house. She gave him an extra dollar tip.

"Hey, doll, how about you keep the dollar and I'll come upstairs with you?"

She took a hot bath, got into bed and turned on the television. When the phone rang at eleven thirty she didn't answer. It rang twice, and then silence. The answering service was on the job. It rang again at one fifteen, waking her from the sleep she had fallen into without having turned off the television. She caught up the phone, her instant thought that something might have happened to Jeff.

"Mrs. Hayes? This is Detective Lieutenant David Marks. I'm sorry to disturb you, but I'd like to see you at your office as soon as you can get here, please. I'll have a police car pick you up."

Julie didn't say anything. She couldn't.

Marks said: "If you'd feel better confirming this call, dial your office when you hang up."

She did. To gain time and composure—or better, to waken herself from the nightmare.

"Lieutenant Marks speaking. Mrs. Hayes?"

"I'll get dressed," Julie said. "Lieutenant, what branch of the police department?"

"Homicide."

SEVEN

A SMALL well-dressed crowd had converged on the barricade near the entrance to the *New York Daily* building—gold and silver slippers, patent leather pumps on the rainy pavement. She preferred to look down, as though looking down might diminish her own high visibility. People were speculating on who she was to arrive under police escort. Everybody on the street seemed to know that Tony Alexander had been murdered. A lot of them were exchanging ideas on why.

On the fifteenth floor the office corridor was cordoned off. *Daily* staffers were trying to convince the police of their priorities. The only acknowledged priorities were those of the Crime Scene unit. Julie was conducted directly into the reception room of Hale and Kister, Architects, across the hall from the Alexander office. The entire area was cloudy with cigarette smoke, the air heavy with the smell of chemicals and wet clothes, and what Julie thought might be gunpowder, but she had not had much experience with that.

A soft-spoken black detective who introduced himself as Wally Herring said he was glad to see her and closed the door on the clamor outside. He had the tape recorder ready to roll when Lieutenant Marks arrived. Marks was good-looking, trim, in his early forties, about six feet. His hair was glossy black and cut with care. His eyes met Julie's as part of a swift non-committal appraisal. He offered his hand, and for a wild minute Julie thought he was going to kiss hers when he lifted it to his nose, and sniffed.

"Yardley's," Julie said, but she felt uneasy.

"We may go to more sophisticated equipment later." He motioned her toward a pair of vinyl upholstered chairs. "Just pick up the volume, Wally." Herring, at the reception desk, adjusted the machine and started it rolling.

"Are you right- or left-handed, by the way?" Marks asked.

"Right," Julie said. "Why the tests?" Since she was sure now that she had smelled gunpowder, the true point to her question was why test *her*.

Marks understood. "Weren't you in the office this evening?" he asked blandly.

"In the building, but not the office."

He looked at her skeptically. "Let's take things in order." He nodded to the other detective.

Herring led her through identification, job description, information on the other staff and a run down on office routine.

"You ought to get the office business from Alice Arthur," Julie said. "She's much closer to Tony and she's been on the job a lot longer than I have."

Marks nodded. "Perhaps you can tell us now what you meant by 'in the building, but not in the office.'"

"I started to sign in at the night desk. Then I noticed Tony's name in the book and decided not to come up."

"Why?"

"It was almost ten o'clock.... No, that wasn't the reason. I just didn't want to see him."

"It was almost ten o'clock," Marks repeated. "Did you think he might have someone in the office with him?"

"I don't think that crossed my mind. I was only thinking of myself."

"So you did not come upstairs?" the detective persisted.

"I did not."

Marks sighed heavily, giving her the impression that he had other information. "So what *did* you do?"

"I went out and caught the first cab I could and went home."

"Do you remember the cabbie's name or number?"

"No, sir. But I think he might remember me—an extra dollar tip to wait until I got inside the building. The phone rang at eleven thirty but I let the answering service pick it up. I woke up alarmed when it rang at one fifteen."

Marks nodded sympathetically, which put her on guard. Which, in turn, was ridiculous. Why should she be on guard? "What was your purpose in returning to the office in the first place, Mrs. Hayes?"

"I did not return to the office, Lieutenant Marks. I intended to look up some names in what we call the celebrity file."

"At ten o'clock at night?"

"Yes." What else could she say?

"When have you been in the office at that hour before?"

"I haven't been."

"You just happened to be in the neighborhood?"

"Could I tell you in my own words what happened yesterday?"

"In your own words. Of course."

Julie recounted her day from Tony's blast at her the moment she entered the office. The tape rolled silently. Marks made an occasional one word note, but he did not interrupt. When she finished he deferred to his partner. Herring asked for Mary Ryan's address and that of Murray's Funeral Home.

"That's a fair walk all by yourself on a rainy night," Marks started again.

"I know."

"How did Phillips die?"

"He's supposed to have jumped from the George Washington Bridge."

"Ah, yes." Then: "Supposed?"

"I believe there was a witness."

He waited a second or so and then asked: "Is there any association in your mind between the two deaths?"

"I don't know."

"That sounds like a qualified yes."

"To explain I have to go back to Wednesday night when my husband and I were having dinner at a restaurant before he left for Europe." She told of Jay Phillips' remarks to her and Jeff. "But I ought to say, Jay's opinion of Tony Alexander was probably shared by a number of people."

"A legion of enemies," Marks suggested.

"A number. It's inevitable in the business."

"Who else do you have in mind?"

Oh, Julie, she thought, never volunteer. "I was just speaking generally, Lieutenant."

"I understand. Have you been able to learn why this Mr. Phillips felt the way he did?"

"No, sir."

"How did Alexander feel about him?"

"Contemptuous is the first word that comes to mind."

"We may want to go into this later," Marks said, "but we must assume for now that Phillips, already dead, is not a suspect in Alexander's murder, which is the crime under our investigation."

"Am I a suspect?" Julie asked.

"Well, you're very much alive," Marks said with the slightest of smiles. "Let's talk some more about you. I understand you and your husband were personal friends of the Alexanders..."

Julie turned that over in her mind: she had scarcely thought of Fran, only of herself. "I ought to have thought about Fran," she said aloud. "We used to be closer friends than we've been lately. I haven't seen her since shortly after I went to work for Tony. He and my husband did meet." She wondered if it was Fran who had told him of the family friendship.

"Did you know she was in the office this afternoon?"

"No, sir."

"Any ill will between you and Mrs. Alexander?"

"Not on my part certainly. I'm fond of her. But the long-standing friendship was between Tony and my husband. Jeff started his career working for Tony."

"Geoffrey Hayes?"

Julie nodded and thought how often she had mentioned him.

"Are you familiar with the box on Alexander's desk, the one with the slot in it?"

"Yes, sir. We put our copy in it for Tony."

"Ever try to get anything out of it?"

"No. I don't think it's possible without the key."

"You know the box is bolted to the desk?"

"I know that I've never seen it in any other place," Julie said, wondering now for the first time why it was so carefully secured.

"Ever see inside of it?"

"Not that I remember."

"Did you know that Alexander kept a loaded revolver in that box?"

"No, sir. I certainly did not know that."

Marks got to his feet. "Let's see if we can go over there now. Wally, anything more you want on the tape from Mrs. Hayes?"

"Mrs. Hayes, did you notice any other name besides Mr. Alexander's in the registry?"

"No. I only noticed Tony's because it was familiar to me."

"Yes, ma'am. What was the name of the man you wrote the story about?"

"Morton Butts."

Marks and Herring exchanged glances. "I'll check it out," Herring said.

EIGHT

JULIE CAUGHT SIGHT of Tim Noble as she moved across the hall with Marks. Herring was waiting for him. Tim looked bereft. Julie wondered why she had no such feeling. She kept wanting to ask, How's Fran? or How's Fran holding up? but even as she framed the words they seemed forced and hollow.

In the office technicians were gathering their gear, repacking their kits at the conference table. Tony's desk was covered with a sheet except for the corner where the copy box had been. There the wood was lighter in color and two holes showed where the bolts had been removed. The floor in the area of the desk and the celebrity bank was marked with masking tape. Chalk circles enclosed dark splotches it took Julie a few seconds to recognize as blood. The shock of reality finally hit home. The room tilted and momentarily went out of focus.

"Are you all right?" Marks asked.

"I'll make it."

When he was sure she was not going to pass out, Marks said, "I thought you might like to look up those names you missed out on last night."

Julie just looked at him.

Marks sighed. "The world is full of s.o.b.s, isn't it?" He echoed Phillips' words to a purpose of his own. "But you do see how hard it is to believe that someone would walk that distance last night in a cold rain?"

"Nevertheless, I did," Julie said.

"Unless the person's mind was on fire, if I can put it that way. And the rejection of a story doesn't seem sufficient motive for that."

"How did you know I came in at all? No name in the book or anything."

"A security officer recognized you, but having recognized you he lost interest and couldn't say what direction you took from the desk."

"Now I understand," Julie said. "Have you reached Alice Arthur?"

"We have," Marks said.

"And Mrs. Alexander?"

He almost seemed amused. "And her daughter."

"I've never met her. I don't even know her name," Julie said.

"Family friends and never met the daughter?"

"She's always been away at school or someplace."

Marks grunted and looked around. The dilapidated leather couch where Tony had claimed to do his best thinking was covered with plastic. A card read: Do not disturb by order of the Police Department. "Would you like to sit down? Perhaps at the table?" The technicians were leaving.

"I'm fine," Julie said.

"Tell me again now: what's in those file drawers?" The whole bank was isolated by movable posts.

"They're profiles of celebrities, or just source material—gossip, rumors, leads.... They're terribly confidential."

"And you wouldn't like to take advantage of access to them now? Who knows when you'll have the opportunity again?"

He was not going to give up until she yielded information that justified her intended visit to the office. "All right. Lieutenant, I wanted to look up Jay Phillips."

"Shall we do it together?"

Naturally.

He cautioned her to touch nothing, especially she was not to touch the cards. The drawers had been examined for prints, but he turned the cards with tweezers. The only entry under Phillips was Ellen Duprey Phillips.

"Wait," Julie said. They both read: "An actress yet. Femme fatale. If you saw her naked you'd say go put some clothes on before you catch cold."

"Any relation?" Marks asked, deadpan.

"She was Jay's wife, and she's been dead for ten years."

"Having caught cold, no doubt," the detective said dryly. "Didn't Alexander ever clean out his files? Ten years—to keep something like that?"

"I think you'd better ask Alice Arthur that question, Lieutenant. I don't know."

"Anyone else while we're here?"

"Morton Butts," Julie said.

"Yes, of course," Marks said. "We must look him up."

"Why?"

He looked up at her from where he was about to tweezer his way through the *b*'s. "You know, Mrs. Hayes, it is customary for the police to ask the questions, not to answer them."

Julie shrugged.

"Because," Marks went on, "there is a name scrawled in the registry downstairs that could be Morton Butts."

"I was wondering whether Tony knew Butts and never let on to me. When I learned at the funeral parlor that Jay Phillips was doing the publicity for this dance marathon, it just didn't make sense. Phillips was a big time public relations man. Why would he take on a two-bit operation on the fringe of Harlem?"

"And one that interested Tony Alexander so that he sent his number one reporter to cover it. How did he find out about it?"

"From a release out of Phillips' office?" Julie suggested. "Alice Arthur might be able to tell us that. I can't really believe he knew Butts. He didn't mention him by name, and Butts seems like an insignificant little man. It was the dance marathon that interested Tony. He'd won a two hundred dollar prize in one when he was young."

Marks continued through the cards to the end of the *b*'s. "No Butts," he said. "But me no buts."

"It wouldn't be hard to remove a card if you wanted to," Julie said.

The detective smiled. He took a piece of chalk from his pocket and marked the drawer. "Who else shall we look up?"

"That's it." Alone, she would have looked up Patti Royce. She would also have looked up the star and the understudy in *Little Dorrit*, but she held back, thinking of the headline possibilities of the merest mention of actors in a hit show.

Marks guided her out of the cordoned area. "I'd like to see your article on Butts and the dance, if you don't mind," he said.

"So would I," Julie said.

"You don't have a copy?"

"Not allowed," Julie said. "Wasn't it in his desk?"

"No, Mrs. Hayes. Nor in the waste baskets, nor in the office. Nor anywhere Miss Arthur could think of."

"She told you about it?"

"She did."

"Boy, she got here in a hurry," Julie said. "All the way from Brooklyn."

"There are investigative facilities in Brooklyn, Mrs. Hayes, and excellent police liaison."

"Oh," Julie said.

NINE

SLEEP CAME, FINALLY, half-way through the four A.M. showing of *Boston Blackie* starring Chester Morris. It was not the picture that tranquilized her. Julie escaped the endless repetitions of the day's trauma by thinking of names she considered unsuitable for an actor: Chester, Elmer, Archibald, Percy.... The phone wakened her at nine. It was Jeff. The first thing she asked was where he was.

"At our Paris office."

"Jeff, do you know about Tony?"

"It came over several hours ago. I thought you might be trying to reach me."

"I was with the police until almost four. Jeff, they even tested me to see whether I'd fired a gun. I haven't ever in my whole life. Did you know Tony kept a gun in the office?"

"I knew he had one, a thirty-eight revolver. Fran has its mate. They belong to a gun club in Queens. But you probably know that."

"I didn't know it," Julie said. "I seem to have known very little about them."

"You'll find that information in the morning paper," Jeff said. "It's in the *Herald* here. They took practice together yesterday afternoon. Do you have anything recent on Fran? I gather she's a prime suspect."

"Is she? I didn't know. Jeff, when you said they were having trouble, did you mean with their marriage?"

"I purposely did not say and I think now it's better to leave it that way."

"Okay," Julie said. "What else did you purposely not say that might help me figure out why Tony was murdered?"

"Is it incumbent on you to participate in the investigation?"

"Jeff, I'm going to hang up on you. What's the matter with you?"

His voice grew even colder. "I'm upset at Tony's death. There ought to have been more I could have done at our last meeting than exchange epithets with him."

"I'm sorry," Julie said. "I didn't know about Fran, only that the police had talked with her and with the daughter. I don't even know the girl's name."

"Her name is Eleanor. I don't know much more about her than you do. She's Fran's daughter by a previous marriage. Tony adopted her as an infant. She'd be twenty-one at least. Tony and Fran were married while I was working for him."

"All I know," Julie said, "is that Fran was visiting her once when I went somewhere with Tony. That's the only mention I ever heard him make of her. Could she be retarded or anything like that?"

"It's possible."

"Didn't Tony ever talk to you about her, for God's sake?"

"Not one word that I can remember."

"That's crazy—like somebody they kept in a closet. Anyway, the police talked with her, wherever she is."

"She's home," Jeff said. "She's the last known person to have spoken with him—on the phone last night."

"I'm sorry I snapped at you," Julie said. "Some crazy things have happened since you left. Besides Tony's death. Can we talk for a few minutes?"

"Take your time. It's on the WATS Line."

"Remember the press agent who came to our table at Sardi's—Jay Phillips?"

"I remember. He had no use for Tony and he'd lost his biggest account—and you know, it skipped through my mind later that Tony might have had something to do with his troubles. But I've interrupted you. What were you going to say about him?"

"He committed suicide a few hours after we saw him." Jeff whistled softly.

"What made you think Tony might have something to do with his troubles?"

"Some pretty free association, I'm afraid. Tony was like a lot of other people with a taste for power, always on the lookout for more. There was something of the bully in him..."

Now he tells me, Julie thought.

She might as well have said it aloud, for Jeff went on: "There was no point in my ever saying this to you. Remember, you asked him for the job yourself, without consulting me. So it was up to you to make your own evaluation and your own adjustment. Tony and I did not become friends until we reached parity, not long before you and I were married. I doubt we'd ever have become close friends if I hadn't acquired a certain reputation of my own."

Jeff always took time to say what he wanted to say, the way he wanted to say it. Much as he wrote. Julie hung on, knowing he would come back to Phillips, and that everything in-between would be relevant. And so it happened. "Now to connect all this to your press agent friend, and the connection is weak, to say the least, one of the Broadway tokens of power Tony coveted in my day was first night tickets." (What he usually got, Julie knew, was second night or preview; only the major critics were sure of opening night.) "Something that came back to me on the plane was having heard Tony on the phone bullying someone for opening night tickets to a show called *Lollopaloozer*. I have a hunch it was Phillips. You ought to be able to look it up if you think it might mean something to you. What I especially remember was his not letting up, a sort of harassment. I was uncomfortable listening to it."

"Jeff, could I try a couple of names on you and see if they ring a bell? ... Morton Butts."

"No, and I think I'd remember that one."

"Ellen Duprey."

"Oh, yes. An actress who gave up the theater to become a nun and after a year or so came out of the convent and took the part of a nun in a play that closed overnight. Don't remember the name of the play. Tony had me interview her,

but he never ran the piece. It irritated him for some reason.
I remember his saying, 'I didn't ask you for *Song of Ber-
nadette*, kiddo.'"

Déjà vu. Of sorts. "Listen, Jeff. Ellen Duprey was married to Jay Phillips. Ten years ago *she* committed suicide,
and Tony used it in the column. Unnecessarily, I'd say.
There is a connection but I've got to find it before I can tell
you where."

"Put a carbon in your typewriter for me."

"I will. How about your work?"

"In progress. Julie, you will go to see Fran, won't you?"

"Of course."

"Please give her my sympathy. I'll write to her myself.
But do what you can for her—for the both of us."

She was tempted to say that she felt it incumbent on her,
for those words from Jeff had stung as no words of Tony's
ever had. But all she said was, "I will."

JULIE WENT DOWNSTAIRS for the newspaper as soon as she
got off the phone. It would have pleased Tony to know that
he had made Page One of the *Times*, she thought upon
seeing it.

From the paper Julie learned that Inspector Joseph Fitzgerald interrogated both Mrs. Alexander and her daughter.
The daughter had failed to reach her mother with a message from Alexander saying that he would be delayed. Alexander returned to the office after attending a cocktail
party at Gracie Mansion. And Mrs. Alexander, after waiting a half hour for him at a midtown restaurant, left and
went directly to her flower shop on Lexington Avenue. The
police reached her there at midnight.

Alexander had been shot at close range, apparently with
his own revolver, but not by his own hand. His body was
discovered shortly after eleven P.M., when the cleaning crew
detected a strong odor of gunpowder outside his office and
alerted the security police.

Julie could almost feel the apartment's quietness; there was not even the usual hum of morning traffic. It was Saturday, she realized, and for a disoriented instant she enjoyed the thought of not having to go into the office. Wake up, Julie. It's nightmare time again.

TEN

THERE HAD BEEN a time when the Alexanders were the only friends of Jeff's whom Julie enjoyed visiting. That was mostly Fran's doing. Fran accepted her in her own right, not simply as Jeff's wife. She sympathized with Julie's assorted failures and tended to discount them as expecting too much of herself too soon. It was to Fran—and only to Fran, outside of Dr. Callahan, that Julie was able to say, *My whole trouble is that Jeff expects too little.* She had been fonder of the Alexander apartment—the penthouse in a turn of the century Park Avenue building—than of her own home. There were plants and books and modern pictures, including a portrait of Tony at his most sardonic, one eye almost closed, at which she always found herself winking back. The memory of those cherished times not so long ago flooded in on her as she went up in the elevator. Even the elevator had used to please her with its little round seats to be lowered from the wall for a leisurely ascent.

People were scattered through the apartment and on the terrace. The sun was shining, a welcome change in weather. A uniformed maid was pouring Bloody Marys.

She found Fran propped up on a chaise longue in the master bedroom accepting condolences. With a shawl over her shoulders and a mohair blanket over her knees, Fran didn't merely look older, she looked elderly. Her face was strained, her hair peppery and dull. When she saw Julie her eyes seemed to brighten and once more Julie wondered at herself for not having seen her for so long. But she did know why: She was not one ever to take the initiative. If Fran had called her she would have come on the instant. Now she waited her turn to speak to her.

The room had been thoroughly tidied, the king-size bed made up as though forever. A great bouquet of red and white carnations stood on the bedside table. From Fran's shop? The shop was called The Basil Pot. She grew herbs as well as plants, buying only her cut flowers on the wholesale market. The Basil Pot was named after a poem by Keats that, as Julie discovered on a reading she could have done without, was pretty macabre: a lover's head is buried in the pot.

Fran took both Julie's hands and pulled her down to kiss her. Her grip was fierce and boney and she held on until she had drawn Julie down beside her on the chaise. She smelled of earth and maybe even of sweat; her fingernails were dirty. Nothing seemed left of the chicness Julie had so admired, and her eyes were tired and bloodshot with no particular color of their own.

"It shouldn't have taken something like this to bring you here," she said, and the tears welled.

"I'm very sorry," Julie said.

"I haven't had much sleep and I don't seem able to stop crying."

"What can I do?" Julie asked.

"There doesn't seem to be anything. It's all been done. Are there police outside, did you notice?"

"I didn't see any. Jeff called from Paris. He's terribly concerned. He wanted you to know."

"I do know," Fran said and smiled a little. "Has he been away for long?" Which showed how much communication there had been between her and Tony.

"Since Wednesday."

"Tony would never go anywhere outside New York."

"Not even Staten Island," Julie said.

"He was afraid his life would turn out to have been a dream, that he'd wake up back on the farm."

"Isn't it crazy," Julie said, "how little we know one another?"

"Ha! Sometimes the more intimate, the less."

People were standing in line waiting to speak to her, but she kept her eyes down to delay acknowledging them. "The police keep coming at me. And at my daughter. I'm surprised we've had this much privacy." She paused and then, as though reminding herself, "I don't think you've met Eleanor, have you?"

"No."

"She's here . . . somewhere."

"I'll find her," Julie said.

"Tom Hastings called this morning." Hastings was the executive editor of the *New York Daily.* "He wanted to know what I thought about having the column go on—perhaps with you and Tim. I said I thought it was a fine idea." She spoke slowly as though an inner clock had run down.

"Thank you," Julie said. She couldn't imagine Tony taking to the idea at all.

"I think you're supposed to call the office. Or Hastings' office. I forget. There will be a message out there."

"I'd better go and let other people have a word with you," Julie said. "It isn't fair not to."

Fran looked up at her. "You still believe in fairness?" Then she gave Julie's arm a squeeze. "You're right, and I may need all my friends. Will you come back this afternoon?"

Julie promised.

She found Eleanor in the guest room and knew her instantly to be Fran's daughter, the set of the eyes, the high, rounded forehead. But the face was longer, the features severe, ascetic-looking. Tall and a bit awkward, the girl was trying to help old Mary Ann Stokes of *The Village Voice* into her coat.

"No flowers," Eleanor said. "He despised flowers unless he could pick them himself." Which was nonsense when you thought about it. Or metaphor: that possibility was intriguing.

"I'll make a donation to the anti-nukes in Tony's name," Miss Stokes said, on her way, "since obviously gun control was not in his purview."

Julie's eyes and Eleanor's met and told that both of them appreciated the gallows humor. When the girl smiled a vein appeared down the center of her forehead. Large dark eyes, no tears, brown hair cut short. She seemed not to know what to do with her hands and finally stuck them in the belt of her jacket.

"You're Eleanor, aren't you? I'm Julie."

The young woman nodded and the vein became even more pronounced.

"I don't know why we haven't met before," Julie said.

"I'm never here for long at a time."

"Are you in school?" Julie found the going difficult.

"Veterinary college. I'm good with animals."

"I'll bet you are," Julie said. "I've heard that's one of the hardest schools to get into."

"Especially Cornell."

"I'm sorry for what's happened here," Julie said.

"Are you?"

Which brought a desultory conversation to a dead halt. "I ought to make a phone call," Julie murmured.

"You're supposed to call the office," Eleanor remembered. "What I meant was that the police have gone away. They were here all night asking the same questions over and over."

"They do that," Julie said.

"Do you think they'll come back again?"

"Until they know what actually happened to Tony, I'm afraid so," Julie said.

"And what if they never find out?"

"I suppose they would go away in time. May I use the phone in here?" It was on a table between twin beds.

"Please," Eleanor said. "Would you like coffee? I'll bring it to you."

"No, thank you."

"I know: orange juice!" So Fran and her daughter had spoken of her.

While Julie was dialing, Kate Wylie of the drama desk came in looking for the bathroom.

Julie pointed to the bathroom door and said, "I hope meeting you at funerals doesn't get to be a habit."

"That's right. We met last night, didn't we? Who'd ever have thought . . ."

Tim Noble answered the phone and Julie turned from Wylie with an apologetic sign. "Where are you, sweetheart?" Tim wanted to know.

"Christ! Don't call me sweetheart. You sound like Tony."

"Sorry, Julie, but I don't know whether I'm high or low. Both. I haven't had any sleep. Hastings wants to see both of us and he isn't going to wait much longer. Please come now before he changes his mind. He wants the column to go on. The police let me in here to wait for your call. It's weird, like a thousand years since I was here last."

"I'm on my way," Julie said.

"Don't walk, for God's sake."

While Julie was amending her lipstick Eleanor brought her a glass of orange juice. "Are you leaving?" the girl said, disappointed.

"I'll come back later, and if there's any way I can help with the arrangements, let me know."

"There won't be any arrangements. Just a messenger with ashes."

Tony, death-size, Julie thought, and felt a chilling brush with reality.

Eleanor drifted from the room when Kate Wylie came out of the bathroom. "Who's that?" Wylie wanted to know.

"Fran's daughter."

"Spooky, isn't she?"

Julie said, "How was Trish Tompkins last night?"

"Marvelous. She *is* Little Dorrit. I intended to give Tony a ring about her. I can't believe he's gone..." Kate took a look at her own faded beauty in the mirror and grappled for her lipstick. "Are you staying on with the *Daily*? You should go see her and remember who told you first, hear?"

"What happened to the original Little Dorrit?"

"Abby Hill. Appendicitis. She'll be going back in in a couple of weeks. Which is why you should go see Trish now."

"Thanks," Julie murmured. What she resolved to do was to find out where Abby was having her appendectomy and visit her.

ELEVEN

In spite of Tim's exhortation, Julie walked. It gave her fifteen minutes in which to contemplate whether or not she wanted a column of her own—half her own. Very few people would think her in her right mind to even hesitate accepting. Tim had called her sweetheart, à la Tony, already into the fantasy. Like Juanita playing teacher. She was aware of the change in herself in the year she had worked on *Tony Alexander Says....* Cynicism was something she had affected in her teens, the epitome of being grown up. But that was a few yesterdays ago and she now considered cynicism a cheap shot, but one she often took just the same.

She kept going back in her mind to her story of Butts and the dance marathon. The police would now ferret out the connection between Butts and Tony, if there was one—among Butts, Phillips and Tony, if there was one. Jeff was probably right: it wasn't incumbent on her...damn him. But whatever the source of Tony's wrath with her, he had raised a question she had to answer: Did you really *gut* care? She had cared more about her smart-ass portrait of Butts. That was the problem. She had felt superior and that simply was not allowed. Then, as though to justify her portrayal of the man as ridiculous, she had grooved on the city real estate. And without having properly done her homework, she had exposed the package to Tony. Jeff, in her position, would have known whether Tony was killing the piece or simply knocking her off the assignment, and he'd have known why. She was about as prepared to carry on a newspaper column as she was to birth a baby.

Tim had already gone down to Tom Hastings' office, a cubby hole off the Editorial Room. Hastings looked like a sportscaster, breezy, sleek hair, tweeds. Electronic apparatus seemed to be seeking communication, but no one paid the slightest attention. Very hard on Julie's nerves, for she was trying without much success to drag herself into the computer age. Miss Page, whose prep school she had attended, kept telling her girls that computers were a fad, like technocracy was when she was their age. Hastings rose and shook hands, as did Tim whose face was flushed all the way to his floppy ears.

"We've got it pretty well worked out if you agree," Hastings said. How was she not going to agree, with Tim's eyes as eager as bubbles and himself about as fragile?

She tried to take in Hastings' outline of the operation: the column would run three days a week instead of Tony's five; to be called *Our Beat* with *Formerly Tony Alexander Says...* in smaller type and their names in still smaller type, Tim's first, he being the senior partner; all copy to be cleared by the Legal Department and then by the city editors; there were other restrictions and qualifications. They were to finish out the month in the fifteenth floor office since Tony had paid the rent, sublet it, and then work among the common folk in the Editorial Room.

"A month's trial, and if it works we'll go to three months. After that we can talk."

Tim explained to her with annoying eagerness that they would be going on at their same salaries.

"How many people your age get an opportunity like this?" Hastings added. "It took Tony years to build his reputation."

Exactly, Julie thought. Who had ever heard of Tim Noble or Julie Hayes? Therefore, why? Why not some established personality? What she said was: "What about a twenty percent cost of living increase?"

Hastings looked offended. "The cost of living hasn't increased that much."

"Ours will."

He laughed, which ought to be worth something, Julie thought.

"And what about Alice Arthur who's been everybody's secretary?"

"She comes out of your cost of living increase."

For one month, for three months . . . Julie still wondered why. Then, as they were leaving his office, Hastings said, "Julie . . . find out what happened to Tony for us."

That put things in a more understandable perspective. And made it incumbent on her to participate in the investigation.

THE POLICE SEAL had been affixed to the Alexander office door. They went across the hall to the borrowed office of Hale and Kister where Lieutenant Marks was going through Tony's appointment book with Alice Arthur. Marks invited them to sit in and contribute anything they thought might be useful.

Alice looked much as she did most days: neat, efficient and so discreet it would make you scream. About the only personal thing Julie knew about her was that she got terrible cramps during her period and took massive doses of Midol for them. Tony had once remarked that he could prescribe something better than Midol. What, Alice had wanted to know. Do you really want me to tell you? Whereupon she had shouted no and burst into tears. Julie was sure Tony had never made a pass at Alice.

Alice kept deferring nervously to Tim or Julie with everything she said. Marks finally interrupted. He proposed to send out for coffee; then, when he looked at his watch he offered hamburgers. It was well past noon.

Alice was on her feet at once. Marks waved her down and put a rookie detective in charge of lunch. He gave him a twenty dollar bill. His attitude had changed since Julie's interrogation. The aggressiveness had toned down. Or maybe he was just tired. Or maybe the suspicion that Fran Alexander was implicated and the fact that a higher echelon detective was in charge there eased the pressure on him.

Julie wanted to know how serious their suspicions were. "I saw Mrs. Alexander this morning," she said.

Marks didn't take the bait.

"Is she really a suspect in Tony's murder?"

Marks looked at her with tired eyes. "If Inspector Fitzgerald says so, Mrs. Hayes."

"Okay."

Marks put his feet up on a magazine table, a copy of *Architectural World* beneath them. "Let's go at it this way," he said. "Let's take it from the top of yesterday and see how it rolls for everybody. Alexander was the first person in the office, right? And that in itself was unusual."

"Unless he slept over on the couch," Alice said. "He did that once in a long while."

"When last?"

"Maybe the night before last, but I'm not sure." She was blushing, but you couldn't tell much from Alice's blushes.

Marks went on: "He was at his desk when you arrived, reading what turned out to be Julie's story."

"Yes, sir."

"Did Alice know he kept a gun in the copy box?" Julie asked.

"Yes," Alice answered for herself. "But the only other person who knew it was Mrs. Alexander."

"To the best of your knowledge," Marks cautioned. "Then Tim arrived. Then Julie; and before she got to her desk he started criticizing the article."

"Alice, do you know what he did with it?" Julie asked. "Did he put it in his pocket, his desk or where?"

"I didn't see. I heard the drawer bang and I took for granted he put it away in his desk, but I didn't look around."

"Much safer," Tim said. "Lot's wife and that sort of thing."

"About eleven," Marks continued, "Julie left and Tim went downstairs with her. When he returned, Alexander gave him a rewrite job. He was still at it when Alexander went to lunch. Alice went shortly afterwards. She returned in forty minutes, at which time Tim gave her some typing and went off to The New York Aquarium to a..." Marks raised his eyebrows. "...Save the Whales luncheon. Alexander came back at two, still in a bad mood, and called Mrs. Alexander to bring the carrying case and her own revolver and pick him up to go for an hour's target shooting. There was discussion about ammunition." Marks, who'd been consulting his notebook throughout, turned to the secretary. "Miss Arthur, give us the phone conversation that followed, as you remember it."

"He said he had a lot of aggression he wanted to get rid of. Mrs. Alexander said something. Then he said, Get your daughter over there. She ought to be good for something besides blackballing me."

Marks took over. "In a half hour or thereabouts Mrs. A. arrived, and when he'd made sure the office door was locked, Alexander opened the desk box, using the key he carried on him, took out the thirty-eight and put it into the twin case. Alice did not observe whether he locked the box during his absence. Probably not, or she'd have noticed his unlocking it on his return."

"I always tried not to look," Alice said.

"At anything?" Tim said.

Marks stepped on his quip. "The Alexanders were gone for two hours. When they got back, the same routine. He locked the door, took the gun from the case and put it into the box. Mrs. Alexander went off with the carrier, her own revolver presumably the one inside. Now suppose Tim or Julie had been in the office, Miss Arthur: what would Alexander have done?"

"He'd have taken the case into the bathroom, removed the gun and kept it in his pocket until everyone had left."

"What was his attitude toward the weapon? Did he like having it? Did it give him pleasure to hold it? Or was he afraid of it?"

"I don't think I can answer that."

Marks went on. "When he returned from the shoot, he was in a better humor. He washed up in your private bathroom, gave Alice his itinerary..."

"Excuse me, sir," Alice said. "You left out that he had me call the Samovar and say that he would cover the nine o'clock show. He wanted the best table in the house."

"Thank you," Marks said and made a note. "The early itinerary checks out as he gave it to Miss Arthur: a brief stop at a theatrical backer's party at Paul's, a motion picture screening at the Eleven Hundred, then to the mayor's birthday party. Shortly after he left the office Miss Arthur locked up and went home early. Well before five.''

"I had his permission," Alice said.

Marks turned to Tim. "Why don't you fill us in from the whale affair on?"

"I was in its belly for three days..."

"Tim," Julie said.

He sighed. "I rode back to Manhattan with Judy Starr in her limousine and did an interview with her on the way. She's decided not to marry that wrestling champ she's been dating. He doesn't dig the whales..."

This time Julie held her tongue. After all, she wasn't his mother.

Tim stretched his skinny neck and his adam's apple gave a bob above the turtleneck sweater. His facetiousness, she realized, owed to the difficulty of bringing himself to say what now came out: "I better give you something here, Lieutenant, which I skipped last time around. I dropped in for a Turkish bath at the Tripod on Thirty-fourth Street. Tony used to go there too: you know, to sweat out tensions." He glanced furtively at Julie. She could not imagine why.

"What time?"

"Four thirty to five thirty. Then I came back here and rapped out the items on the whales and Miss Starr, deposited them in the copy box and took off for the seven o'clock opening of *Murder Money*. After that it was the opening night party at Pier Fifty-two, which takes me through till one A.M."

Julie wondered what he was doing at an opening; that he would lay out his own money was out of the question. Somebody's guest, probably, somebody whose name would show up in an item for the column.

Marks said that Tim's copy had gone to the lab with the copy box. "Which brings us back to where we started: What has become of Julie's story? If he put it in his pocket and carried it around with him, why was it not on his person when the police arrived? Who would he have given it to?"

"Morton Butts," Julie suggested.

"Or who would have taken it without his leave?"

"Same answer," Julie said.

"According to Alice's best recollection," Marks said carefully, and Julie noted that he had now gone on a first name basis with all of them, "it was the ending of that story that enraged Alexander, the straw that broke the camel's back."

"That's what it seemed like to me," Alice said, somewhat flustered as though she had finked on Julie. "I could be wrong."

"And you could be right," Julie snapped. Then, to the detective: "I felt there might be some political maneuvering behind the Garden of Roses lease to Butts."

"I'd have thought that would interest someone like Alexander," Marks said, leading the witness.

Julie leaped ahead rather than seem to fall into a trap. "I hoped it would, but I should have researched it better. Instead, I went to a quick source that may have angered Tony—my going to him instead of doing my own homework."

"May we know who you went to?" Marks asked blandly.

Julie hesitated, remembering her promise to Romano that her source was sacred, a promise given, however, outside the context of Tony's death. Before answering she turned to Alice: "Did you feel that Tony knew where I'd got my information? Not information. My questions?"

"Yes."

Tim blew everything open. "For God's sake, Julie, even I knew it had to be Sweets Romano."

"Yes, I suppose so," Julie said.

"I mean who else do you know who has a handle on everything including West Side real estate?"

Julie nodded and glanced at Marks. "You know who Romano is?"

"Oh, yes," Marks said, very dry. "I don't know what we'd do in our business without him."

"I have this crazy kind of rapport with him that I don't really understand myself."

"No need to explain. We all need our informants."

Julie knew better than to offer further explanation. Besides, there wasn't any. "Lieutenant, could we find out if Morton Butts was at the Gracie Mansion party. In the interview he said he expected the mayor to attend the opening of the dance marathon. I thought he was kidding. Now I wonder."

"We already know that he was there," Marks said. "What we'd better find out now is on whose invitation. I doubt, from your description of him, that it came directly from the mayor."

"The trouble is I'm beginning to doubt my description of him."

Marks phoned the mayor's office and spoke to someone called Maggie.

They were finishing their hamburgers when Marks got a call he expected to be from Maggie. It was not. From his responses Julie deduced that it was from his boss. Alice gathered the napkins and paper cups. Tim was composing something in longhand.

Marks sat a moment thinking after he hung up the phone. Then he dialed his own headquarters and asked if Herring had come on duty yet. Apparently not. "Who's in?" he asked, and from the names mentioned chose a detective called Tomasino and asked that he meet him at a Park Avenue address Julie recognized as the Alexanders'.

Marks turned off the tape recorder and pocketed the tape.

"What about your call to the mayor's office?" Julie asked.

"She knows where to leave a message for me."

He was going out the door when Julie said, "Thanks for the hamburgers, Lieutenant."

He looked back and grinned. "My pleasure. Her name is Maggie Taylor. Tell her I said she could give you the message. It might work. If it does, we'll call it a *quid pro quo*, shall we?"

"Okay," Julie said, but she wondered: for favors past or in the future?

TWELVE

WHEN MARKS LEFT THEM Julie told Alice what had taken place in Hastings' office. She said she wasn't sure the column could afford a secretary after the first of the month.

"I don't want to work for just anybody," Alice said.

"'Just anybody' might turn out to be a good guy," Tim said.

"Alice," Julie said, "was Tony a good guy?"

"How do you mean?"

She cast about in her mind for a way to illustrate. "If he was your father, would you have been proud of him?"

"I often did think of him as my father, and I was more afraid of him than anything else."

"That makes two of us."

"Three," Tim said.

Alice folded her hands over the borrowed typewriter. "I suppose a lot of people would say he was not a good person. He was suspicious of everybody. When something humane or philanthropic about a person came in, he would say, 'Let's find out why they're doing it. What's in it for them?'"

"She's right," Tim said. "Tony didn't trust success, even his own. He just worshipped it—like one of those ancient gods or goddesses you had to keep paying tribute to... or else." He drew his finger across his throat.

"You knew him better than any of us, Alice. What went wrong with him lately that turned him so mean?"

"He wasn't mean with me," she said. A clam.

"Then why were you scared of him?"

"Because I was scared of my own father when he was alive."

Julie saw no point in going round and round on that one. She turned to Tim and said, with an edge: "The same Turkish bath. The Tripod: what does that mean?"

"Three. Where they're not a crowd," Tim said.

"Oh."

"It's better than Eighth Avenue, sweetheart."

"Okay."

"You asked."

"Oh, damn it, I know I did."

Alice said, "Not lately. I mean Tony wasn't there lately."

"How can you be sure?" Julie asked.

"I just am."

Tim said, "I don't know which of you is more naive."

"Me," Julie said.

"It means he was getting what he wanted somewhere else," Tim said.

And still Alice sat, almost prim, tight-lipped.

"I'm beginning to get the picture," Julie said. What she was wondering was if Jeff knew about the Tripod, and if he did, what?

"Julie, if you don't find out what happened to Tony—or if the police don't solve this murder soon, do you think Hastings will fold the column?"

"I think it will depend on the column. You've got to believe that, Tim."

Did she believe it herself? Yes, deep down. They were on sufferance, and what Hastings was looking for most was an immediate investigative job—in which pursuit Julie had some small credit—and the sensational copy it might spark. Tony's death shouldn't be a total loss. Or, more kindly, the *Daily*, like every tabloid, needed all the hype it could get.

THEY BEGAN THEIR FIRST collaborative column with the lead: "Tony Alexander died at his desk Friday night." They pasted up three columns from copy Tony had cleared for future use. Julie wrote again as best she remembered it her piece on Butts and the dance marathon, not to use, but to have approximately as Tony had read it. She cringed at the opening. It triggered a replay of Tony reading the whole damn thing aloud. Hard on the ego, not so bad for the memory.

"Julie..." There was a confessional tone to Tim's voice. She looked around. "I picked up a cute item on one of the kids in *Murder Money*. He used to be a jockey only he started growing again at the age of twenty. It ruined his career on a horse. Okay with you to run it?"

"Why? I'm not saying not to. I'm just saying ask yourself why. Is it good for the column or a personal favor?"

"Shit," Tim said. Then, "You're right, but don't go being right all the time."

The call came from the mayor's office: "Maggie Taylor for Lieutenant Marks, please." A strong feminine voice.

Julie, identifying herself, persuaded her that Marks intended to share the information.

Maggie Taylor thought it over for a second. Then: "The subject attended the party with Councilman Daniel McCord who first cleared it with the mayor's secretary."

Julie repeated the name as she wrote it. "McCord's famous for something, isn't he?"

"He's the organizer of 'Save the family, save the neighborhood, save the city.'"

"Is Morningside Heights and environs one of the neighborhoods he wants to save?"

"That's his district."

"I ought to be able to find him in the phone book," Julie said. "Thank you very much..."

Mrs. Taylor interjected, "It's Daniel Matthew McCord. They've nicknamed him Damn McCord in the chamber. I don't know the address, but he owns a bicycle shop on Amsterdam Avenue."

"Thank you," Julie said again. "I'll pass the information on to Lieutenant Marks."

"So will I," Mrs. Taylor said.

When Julie hung up the phone Alice Arthur said, "I wish I could stay on with the column."

"One day at a time, but let's work on it."

On her way out Julie stopped at the *Daily* library and looked up *Lollopaloozer*, the musical Jeff had heard Tony

demanding opening night tickets for. The newsprint had
started to crumble before they got it on microfilm, but she
made out that it opened nineteen years ago in November
and that Michael Dorfman was the producer. If Jay Phillips handled the publicity, Jeff was right: he was the one
Tony had talked tough to. And he had got the tickets: a
paragraph in the next day's column began, "In our fifth row
seats at the opening of *Lollopaloozer* we could hardly see
the stage for the stars in our eyes . . ."

And he had gagged on "I never promised you a rose garden."

THIRTEEN

JULIE TOOK the Lexington Avenue subway uptown and walked from the Eighty-sixth Street stop to Murray's Funeral Home. Be it ever so humble it was a busy place, getting everybody underground before the Sunday layoff. She persuaded the person on office duty to let her belatedly sign the Phillips memorial book. It was about to be packaged with other mementos for the Phillips sisters. Julie's hunch paid off: D. M. McCord and M. Butts had both attended the viewing. They had signed in early—Butts' signature looking like a series of M's with a line through. They could have walked from Murray's to Gracie Mansion. Julie thought about signing a false name, but she didn't. She paid respect.

Afterwards she took the crosstown bus through Central Park and walked up Amsterdam Avenue. She passed the Garden of Roses, closed up tight as a drum. No registration going on, no renovations. But then it was Saturday as well as the day after Tony Alexander's murder.

SHE WAITED FOR MCCORD to finish with a customer who wanted an old-fashioned bicycle, one you could brake by standing up on the pedals. McCord's son, a sandy-haired boy who bore a strong resemblance to his father, drew the grille across the entryway. It was getting on toward six and a lot of other merchants on the street were doing the same thing. McCord promised to call the customer if the kind of bike he wanted came his way. He walked the man to the door and turned to Julie.

"Yes, ma'am. What can I do for you?" His very blue eyes were friendly, curious. You could tell he liked people.

"I'm not sure," Julie said, explaining who she was and why she was there. "I'd like to run a piece on Mr. Butts and the dance marathon, but I wanted to check with you first."

McCord bade his son lock up and sweep the front of the store. He took Julie to the back room where they could sit down. He gave her the desk chair and settled himself astride a two-step ladder. "Now. How did you get to me?"

"I saw both your names in the book at the funeral parlor and I know you went to the mayor's birthday party together."

"But why check with me instead of Butts himself?"

"I'm curious to know how he managed to lease the property from the city."

"And he refuses to tell you?"

She could feel herself slipping into a defensive position, those righteous eyes of his seeking truth. "I haven't asked him. It didn't occur to me at the time of the interview and I haven't been able to reach him since."

"You don't trust him, is that it?"

"I'm not saying that exactly. I just didn't think he was for real, to tell the truth. But when I found out Jay Phillips was doing his publicity, it put a different light on things."

"I begin to see—or am I wrong? You're trying to find out if there's a connection between Jay's suicide and Butts' deal with the city for the Garden of Roses."

"You're dead wrong, sir. Such an idea never crossed my mind. What I'm most interested in are the deaths of two men who didn't like one another—Tony Alexander *and* Jay Phillips. Is there a connection in their deaths? I don't know, but I'd like to find out. And whether Mr. Butts comes into the picture at all, I don't know. But I'm trying to find that out too. And we will run something in the column about his dance marathon if it comes off, but I would like to know more about the real estate deal first."

"Fair enough," McCord said, Julie having met his challenge. "I think I can clarify that for you. Whether you want to blow it up into some sort of scandal is your business. From what I've read in *Tony Alexander Says . . .* I think that's what he might have done with it. A little distortion of facts never troubled a gossip monger. Sorry if that offends you.''

Julie shrugged.

''You see, I don't think there's a dishonest buck in the whole deal. And it started in my back yard. My folks and the Phillips family have been friends since before I was born. We all belong to the same parish. My mother and Miss Eileen and Mary Jean went to parochial school together over fifty years ago. I attended Jay's wake on behalf of my mother who's laid up with a broken hip. And while I was there the sisters asked me if I could get Mr. Butts next to Mayor Bracken, that Jay had promised him. I wasn't going to get a better opportunity than right then, so I took him along with me to the mayor's birthday party. The fact is I was already pretty well acquainted with Mr. Butts. About six months ago Jay came into the shop here and asked if I could do anything about getting a friend of his a long lease on the Garden of Roses. I looked into the matter. The property belongs to the city and the building was condemned, about to be torn down. But in the meantime, the University was stirring around to get the best deal possible on it.''

The bus garage idea was apparently before his time, thought Julie. Otherwise what he was saying jibed with the information Romano had given her.

''Now you may not know it, ma'am, but it's my philosophic belief and my geographic cure for some of the ills of the city that we can save it by saving the neighborhoods, and I'm by no means convinced that having chunks of city real estate gobbled up by the university complex is going to save the neighborhood for the people who live there. I'm an advocate of the small, privately owned business that services its own community. And I had a feeling that Mr. Butts might come up with something enterprising, and the very least that could happen, I figured, was he'd hold the property in place, you might say, till we see what happens to that wasteland to the east of it.

''For another thing, if Jay Phillips had faith in him, and I know for a fact that he did—he co-signed eighty thousand dollars' worth of notes, which is a fair amount of faith by my arithmetic—it was high enough recommendation for me. So, to make a long story short, I went to this city board and that one, and the deal went through. As I said before, I don't think there's a dishonest penny anywhere down the line. Not everybody could renovate a building for eighty thousand dollars these days, and not everybody'd want to renovate that one. But if anybody asks you what a dance pavilion's doing on a million dollar property that belongs to the city, you ask them about the millions and millions of dollars' worth of city property with nothing sitting on it but a burnt-out shell of bricks.''

"I see what you mean," Julie said, and thanked him for talking so frankly with her.

McCord got up when she did. "I talk straight, Mrs. Hayes. Sometimes I talk too much like most politicians, but you can count on it being straight.''

"Did you meet Tony at the mayor's party?"

"No. Didn't really want to, to tell the truth. When he came in Butts went straight up and introduced himself. By then he was on his own. I congratulated the mayor and went home to my supper.''

"Did Butts recognize Tony himself?"

"His picture's been running in the paper every day for as long as I can remember," McCord said.

"Yes, of course," Julie said. Back at square one again.

FOURTEEN

A GREAT CHANGE had come over the Alexander apartment in a few hours. A woman Julie didn't recognize opened the door. The place looked trampled through or as though an auction had been held there with everything sold in place and now waiting to be carted away. The doors off the foyer, generally open, were closed. The woman was a detective, Julie realized as she followed her to the dining room—a solid person in a dark blue suit and carrying a shoulder bag. The remains of a buffet meal lay on the long table, the salads wilted, the butter soft, cold meats beginning to curl and discolor. Luncheon plates, some with the food on them scarcely touched, had been returned to the table. A big man with luminous eyes and hearty mustache came to meet them.

Detective Jane Lawler introduced herself and her partner, Joe Ferretti.

Eleanor rushed from the kitchen and then stopped with almost comic abruptness.

Julie looked at the detectives: they were tensed as though ready to intervene if the girl had gone further.

"Something's happened here since this morning. What?"

"They've taken mother away. I don't know what they're going to do about me."

The detectives had nothing to say.

Julie put her carry-all on a chair and suggested to Eleanor that they clean up.

"I've been trying, but I don't seem to get anywhere."

When everything from the table was in the kitchen, Eleanor closed the door. Detective Lawler opened it and set the doorstop in place. She and her partner sat in the chairs nearest the kitchen. There was nothing to do but ignore them. "Do you know where your mother is?" Julie asked.

"She went to the shop with Inspector Fitzgerald and some other detectives. Some of them stayed here and started questioning people. Everybody cleared out so fast you'd have thought it was a bomb scare."

"Then what?" Julie put the meats and cheeses on one plate and covered it with plastic wrap.

"It got down to them and me." She indicated the detectives who were dividing a newspaper between them. "They kept getting a lot of gibberish over their intercom system and then Detective Lawler asked me to fix an overnight bag for my mother which the police would pick up. I don't know where she is and if they know they won't tell me."

Julie's guess was that the trip to the shop had to do with the other revolver, the mate to Tony's. Except that they would have picked that up the night before, suspecting that the guns might have been switched. "I assume she's been in touch with her lawyer?"

"Yes. He telephoned me and said I wasn't to talk with anyone unless he was present. But that doesn't mean you."

"It might," Julie said. She scraped the dishes, rinsed them and handed them one at a time to Eleanor to put in the dishwasher.

"If only I knew where mother was I'd be more together, you know?"

"I'll see if I can find out," Julie said. "Do you know the lawyer's name?"

"I forget his name. He was Tony's lawyer."

"Then I can find out through the office."

"If I need a lawyer will you find one for me?"

That seemed strange from a couple of angles. Julie looked at the girl, who was avoiding her eyes. "Do you expect that to happen?"

"Yes."

"Do you want to tell me why?"

"I can't prove where I was last night. Mother told the police I was here, but I wasn't actually. I went to a movie. I went to see *Stevie* again."

Again, Julie noted. "Same theater?"

Eleanor nodded. "I always cry. It's so beautiful."

"I know."

"You saw it?"

Julie said that she had.

"I love the aunt more than any character I've ever seen in any picture," Eleanor said.

Julie put the detergent into the machine. She sneezed several times.

Detective Lawler called out, "God bless you."

"Thank you." She remembered the cold she had thought she was getting. Aborted. "The police will find someone who saw you at the movie, Eleanor."

"Not necessarily."

"If you were there."

Eleanor finally looked at her. Was the girl trying to build a case against herself? She had shed no tears for Tony, not in Julie's presence. "Julie, would you stay here with me tonight?"

"I'm not sure I can. I've got things I must do."

"Night clubs and previews and things like that?"

"None of those things. They're not important right now."

"Are they ever?"

"Yes, relatively and sometimes." The dishes were in the machine helter-skelter, big plates, little ones, cups, more plates, glasses.... She began to rearrange them.

"What difference does it make how they're arranged?" Eleanor wanted to know. "A dishwasher is not a work of art."

Julie pondered this a moment and then closed the washer door and sent the machine on its way. The dining room table hadn't been a work of art either. She made a pot of coffee. Eleanor sat on a stool and watched her. Neither of them spoke. When the coffee was ready she poured herself a cup and then took some out to the detectives. Eleanor said she never drank coffee. When Julie proposed to make a few phone calls, the girl asked if anyone minded if she lay down for a while. Nobody did, but when she went through the foyer and on to the guest room, turning on lights as she went, Detective Lawler followed and lugged along a chair from the foyer which she set down opposite Eleanor's room. Again, when the girl closed the door the detective opened it.

Julie turned to Ferretti who had joined the procession. "Is she not to be left alone? How come?"

He opened the living room door and beckoned Julie to follow him. She waited while he found the light switch. When the lights came on she saw what he had brought her in to see: the portrait of Tony hung in strips, slashed through.

"Did she do it?"

"She sure did."

"When?"

"A couple of hours ago. My partner and I were having a bite to eat out there."

Strange to do it now, Julie thought, with the man already dead. She asked the cop for an opinion: "Real or acting, do you think?"

"It's some kind of real no matter what."

Julie stayed in the living room to make her calls. Service first. Saturday night: she reached no one by phone except Alice Arthur whose mother called her from the kitchen where she was doing dishes. How many men were doing dishes at this hour, Julie wondered in a sudden burst of irrationality. She got the attorney's name from Alice: Allan Zimmerman. Was Allan Zimmerman washing dishes? She marched out to the kitchen with her empty coffee cup. Joe Ferretti was at the sink washing his and Detective Lawler's cups and saucers.

FIFTEEN

"But why?"

Eleanor, her back against the headboard, drew up her knees and clasped her hands around them. "I don't know, except that it made me furious to look at it, that same superior sneer. And they'd taken mother away without any explanation. The paper knife was lying on the table. I hated Tony. There's no secret about that."

"Not now anyway," Julie said. "How do you think Fran's going to feel?"

"I haven't let myself think about that."

"All right," Julie said. "It's done."

"Would you have taken it away if I'd asked you to?"

"It's Fran's picture, Eleanor. Not yours and certainly not mine. But to answer your question, no. I had my own troubles once, getting rid of a portrait I didn't like." Julie thought back: hours of agony over the subject, but the idea of destroying it had never crossed her mind.

"What did you do about it?" Eleanor wanted to know.

"About two years of psychiatry. But it was the picture I hated, not what it represented. Actually, it was the artist, but I didn't know it at the time. It was a portrait of my husband painted by his first wife."

"You think I've done something terrible, don't you?"

Julie shrugged. "Have you always felt this way about Tony?"

"For as long as I can remember."

"Do you know why?"

"Oh, yes. And it wasn't because my mother loved him more than she did me."

"It wasn't," Julie said skeptically.

"I know: There are different kinds of love." That
sounded like a quotation and it was. "Mother took me to a
child psychiatrist, but I wouldn't talk to him."

"That's one place you don't get very far if you don't talk.
Not that I'm all that sure you get someplace when you do
talk. It depends on the individual—and faith."

"Do you believe in God?"

"Yes."

"I don't think I do and I've been trying all my life."

Julie kicked off her shoes and folded her legs into the lo-
tus position, sitting on the other bed. Detective Lawler returned to her chair in the hallway, having used the bathroom
off the master bedroom. "I don't think it's something you
get by trying," Julie said, "and whatever I believe in isn't a
literal being—no long white beard or anything like that."

"Or dirty white mustaches?" Eleanor said.

Julie didn't say anything.

"Where do you suppose mother is?"

"We'll hear from her soon," Julie said, wishing she felt
as confident as she tried to sound. When she had called Allan Zimmerman's Eightieth Street residence all she learned
was that he was with a client.

"You won't even say where you think she is?" Eleanor
asked.

"I think she's with the police, but I think she'll be home
tonight."

"Then what about the overnight bag?"

"I don't know what that means." But it implied a lot of
possibilities that she wasn't going to sort out in front of
Eleanor: for one, that Fran was being held without bail,
which meant that she had been arraigned.

"Do you know what I think?" Eleanor said. "Asking me
to pack a bag for her was psychological warfare. Meant to
intimidate me. They think I'll break down and confess. I'm
the one they really suspect."

"That's pretty subtle of them," Julie said. "Did you have
the opportunity? That's one of the first questions."

"Yes. I knew he was back at the office. If nobody saw me at the movie they could say I wasn't there. After all, I'd seen the picture before so I knew what it was all about. I knew when the show went on, and about the musical interlude."

"Eleanor, what are you trying to do?"

"Maybe I *was* the one who killed him. People do things and then black out."

What she was trying to do, Julie reasoned, was to draw attention away from her mother. And that suggested the girl's own fear of her mother's guilt. The destruction of Tony's portrait could be a deliberate attempt to draw suspicion on herself. If Eleanor had killed him, the picture business would have been anti-climactic, the need for violence sated. Or would it? Coming home to Tony as large as life, as real as Banquo's ghost, and at his most malevolent if that was how you saw him. The portrait did have a satanic quality, which was what Tony liked best about it.

After a few seconds Eleanor said, "Tony wasn't my real father. My father was killed just after mother and he were divorced. He was killed in a plane crash in the Egyptian desert."

And had become a legend, Julie thought, even as her own father had. It was a subject on which they could talk for hours and probably never come near the truth.

"I was a year old. Mother must have felt very guilty about the divorce. She'd been raised a Catholic and the Church was stricter then. When my father died, she felt it was God's vengeance on her for wanting to marry Tony."

"Is this your version or Fran's?"

"She wouldn't admit it, not to me anyway. Don't misunderstand. I love my mother...except when she makes me hate her."

Love-hate: Julie thought of the hours she had spent on Doctor Callahan's couch trying to associate her way into understanding how she felt about her own mother.

"Didn't Tony adopt you, Eleanor?"

"Yes."

"So he must have cared about you."

"He wanted mother to think so. What I remember most about him when I was small was me trying to get even with him for hurting me. He'd step on my foot—hard—and then pretend it was accidental. Or pull my hair and pretend it was caught in the buttons of his cuff. When I said he hurt me on purpose, mother didn't believe me. It wasn't until I started making things up about him that she really listened to me. They were horrid things, mostly pertaining to the bathroom. It's all so disgusting."

"It's symptomatic," Julie said. "It means something."

"Then you believe me?"

"Yes." She did believe that the girl herself thought Tony had hurt her on purpose.

"When I was seven they sent me to live with my grandmother, I kept thinking about her when I saw the picture *Stevie*. If Granny had lived we could have been like that, and I do write poetry although it isn't very good. I loved Granny and the farm from the first minute. But she got sick and the farm had to be sold and when I was ten I was sent to boarding school. I've been away at school or summer camp ever since. With tiny little duty visits from mother.

"I used to pretend to myself that the reason she stayed with Tony was because he provided money to take care of me, but she started The Basil Pot with her inheritance from Granny and made lots of money herself.... Did you ever read a poem called *Isabella, or the Basil Pot*?"

"Morbid," Julie said.

Eleanor smiled, a tight, wicked little smile, so that Julie could envision the child who made up stories about her stepfather. A child's vengeance: It was something that would forever fascinate her. That was truly the loss of innocence, more surely than the instance of a child's victimization.

"It isn't that I didn't try to like Tony or to make him like me. I'd come here summers sometimes, but after a week or so it just didn't work. All this sounds as though I'm sorry for myself. I'm not, but I do take myself too seriously. You were right."

Someone else must have said that, Julie thought, but she let it pass. She unfolded her legs.

"Please don't go."

"I ought to," Julie said. "I was hoping Fran would come before I had to leave."

"A little while longer," Eleanor pleaded. Then an instant reversal: "Oh, damn it, go if you have to. I hate myself when I beg."

Julie slipped off the bed and into her shoes. "We all beg sometimes. You shouldn't hate yourself."

"I feel like a child when I do it. I think of myself as a child, ugly, dirty-minded and whiny, something even a mother couldn't love."

"Maybe once you were an ugly duckling," Julie said, "and you know what happened to her."

"Was it a her?"

"Why not?"

Eleanor smiled. Her face was beautiful then, her eyes warm, intelligent. Julie held her hand out to her, her left hand to be clasped sidewise. Eleanor lifted it to her cheek, then brushed it with her lips.

Julie kissed the top of her head. Eleanor's vein grew prominent in her shyness and need for affection. "What are you doing here in New York?" Julie asked. "Hasn't school started?"

"Yes, but when Tony called and said my mother needed me, I got here as fast as I could."

"When?"

"He called on Tuesday and I got here Wednesday. And wouldn't you know, mother was furious? With *me*."

"And did she need you?"

"Not so that she'd admit it at first.... Julie, can *she* hear me?" She nodded toward the detective.

"I doubt it. Just keep your voice down."

"I'd kill myself if I thought they were using me to get information about mother."

"I don't think that's what they're about," Julie said and sat down on the edge of Eleanor's bed.

"Mother did need me even though she hated the idea. Tony didn't come home at all Thursday night and I was there when she fell apart and the whole thing spilled out about Tony and this girl. But the way she told it...like it was something she didn't think was real, a male menopause fantasy. Isn't that something?"

"It happens," Julie murmured almost under her breath.

"He was going to leave her, Julie. And the bastard used me to hold her up so he could get away. He wanted a divorce. She told me how she tried to follow him sometimes, to catch them together, and then she would run away at the last minute. She felt so humiliated she could have died."

"Do the police know about this, Eleanor?"

"Maybe that's why they took her away."

"Did she know the person he was involved with?"

"I don't think so. She said she didn't want to know because it wasn't going to last."

And yet she had tried to follow them. Poor Fran, Julie thought. Then: did Jeff know? Did Alice Arthur know? It was Alice who'd said Tony hadn't been at the Tripod lately. And Tim who had explained why: He was interested elsewhere. Did Tim know? She thought back to Thursday night: that was the night Alice said she thought he had stayed in the office. It was the night she herself had been there polishing the Butts story until almost eight. If Tony had returned he'd have had to sign in, and there would be a record.

If Tony had planned to leave Fran—and had called Eleanor home to be with her mother—then when, exactly had he intended to make the move? Had the whole scheme suddenly fallen apart on him? Target practice with Fran and a planned late dinner and show? If that wasn't reconciliation, what was it?

"Eleanor, wouldn't Fran have felt things were coming round in her favor yesterday? The dinner date and all?"

"And then what happened? He called to say he'd be an hour late and wanted Fran to know. He wanted me to call her. Why couldn't he do it himself?"

"There must have been a reason."

"There was. There was a woman with him in the office. I could hear whispering in the background.

"Have you told this to the police?"

"I don't think they believed me."

"She'd have had to sign in on the ground floor of the building," Julie said.

"Not if she got there early enough."

"That's so," Julie said. It sounded as though Eleanor might have reconnoitered. "Did Tony know you heard a voice in the background?"

"Probably."

"Did you confront him with it? Did you tell him you heard the whispering?" And how could you tell the sex of a whisperer, Julie wondered.

"Certainly not. I didn't want him using me."

"For what?"

Eleanor threw out an impatient hand. "He wanted a divorce, didn't he? I didn't want him calling on me for a witness."

As Julie took her departure, hearing the hollow clack of her heels reverberate through the silent apartment, she thought of the number of times Eleanor had spoken of being used. It would take even a Doctor Callahan years to work her way through Eleanor's labyrinthine mind.

She was waiting for the elevator when Detective Lawler opened the door that Julie had just closed behind her. "Mrs. Hayes, Lieutenant Marks would like you to wait downstairs in the lobby till he gets here. He'll be here in a few minutes."

SIXTEEN

"GIVE ME ten minutes upstairs?" Marks said on arrival. "Then I need your help on a few questions."

"Where's Mrs. Alexander?" Julie asked before committing herself.

"She'll be home within the hour. Have you had dinner?"

"Is she out on bail or what?"

"You're so dramatic," Marks said mockingly. "There have been no arrests in the case as of this hour. How's that?"

"It will have to do," Julie said. Then: "I haven't had dinner yet."

"Then wait for me in that Volvo out front and think of someplace in the neighborhood that's not too fancy."

The doorman opened the car door for her. It was a glossy black monster of bustle vintage. The doorman stood a moment in admiration. "You don't see many of these anymore, not in this condition. It reminds me of my Aunt Mary." He patted his buttocks to show the area of association.

An early edition of Sunday's *Daily* was on the seat. The headline read: *Alexander Murder a Family Affair?* In the semi-darkness she was able to read only the heading of the page three story: *Switch of Weapons at Gun Club Possible*.

Julie closed her eyes and improvised a possible scenario: Assume the revolvers have been identified as *his* and *hers* by the registration numbers on the permits. Say Fran and Tony each tried out the other's gun during practice. Mixed up fingerprints on both. Back at the office, while Tony locks the door and opens the copy box, Fran takes out her revolver—whether by design or accident—and hands it to Tony. He stores it away, etc. If Fran switched the guns intentionally, she could have returned with his gun, killed him, and left the weapon wherever the police had found it. She would then have unlocked the copy box with Tony's key and taken her own gun back to the shop with her. Premeditated murder.

No, no, no. She turned her mind to Eleanor's story and the case she seemed to be trying to make against herself. Tony, unless the murderer entered the office with him, would have had to open the door to his assailant—someone he either knew or expected. And if that person did not bring the murder weapon with them, Tony must have opened the copy box some time in there and taken out his own revolver. In anticipation of what? And under those circumstances, how had his assailant got hold of the gun?

Marks climbed into the car before the doorman could get round to his side.

"The Galway Bay," Julie said. "It's not too far." She gave him the address.

"Why is that familiar to me? I don't think I've been there."

"It's where I went to dinner with Mary Ryan last night— before we went to the funeral parlor next door."

"Ah, yes." He slipped the purring Volvo into gear. "You were right about your Mr. Butts going to the mayor's party, weren't you?"

"With City Councilman McCord. I went to see him this afternoon. He engineered the Garden of Roses deal—a favor to Phillips in the beginning. Old family friends."

"But kosher," Marks said.

"Apparently."

"Don't be disappointed. The only way to find the bad guys is to sort out the good guys."

"I guess," Julie said. "If the councilman's right, as soon as Butts found out who Tony was at the party, he introduced himself to him. Then what?"

"Alexander invited him to the office to discuss the promotion of the marathon dance and what he could do to help."

"At that hour? And when he was supposed to meet Fran?"

"He had to go back to the office for a reason which was probably not Butts. Allow the little man some exaggeration to add a few inches to his stature."

"He needs them.... Lieutenant, I don't believe Tony was that much interested in him and his whole set-up."

Marks shook his head at her persistence.

"I guess I'm not qualified to judge that," Julie said.

"As far as the police are concerned, we know Alexander went back to the office when he probably had not intended to, and when he got there he phoned a message to be passed on to Mrs. Alexander that he was delayed for an hour. According to Butts, Alexander kept him there longer than Butts wanted to stay. He was late arriving at his next destination. But he did arrive—among a crowd of witnesses, so that his alibi for the time of Alexander's death is solid."

"A crowd of witnesses?" Julie picked up.

"He went uptown to a Saturday night prayer meeting at Brother Joseph's Temple." Marks braked for a traffic light. He looked at Julie. "How does that fit in with your notion of Mr. Butts?"

"It fits." Julie thought of the bible on Butts desk. "He'll get Brother Joseph to preach the marathon. That'll bring 'em in. I did a profile on Brother Joseph once. He believes that money is a divine grace."

"Amen!" Marks said. Then: "Butts arrived at the temple in time for the hour of witnessing."

"Pretty obvious, isn't it?" Julie said.

"Well, yes. He discussed your story with Alexander, by the way. Alexander gave it to him to read, but not to keep. It was on the desk when Butts left. If he's telling the truth."

"Of course he's telling the truth, a man of God."

Marks made a sound of reproach. They turned onto Third Avenue. They were almost there.

It occurred to Julie that she had just sounded remarkably like Tony.

"I'D FORGOTTEN ABOUT the Irish and Saturday night," Julie said when Marks slid into the booth opposite her. The bar was jammed. Several earnest conversations were going on at high decibel, about politics and politicians, local appointments, the New York Mets, and how things were going on the other side of the ocean. An enlarged photograph hung at the opposite end of the bar to the television set. Having given it some thought before, Julie realized that it was Bobby Sands, the I.R.A. martyr who had starved himself to death in prison.

"Your friend Mrs. Ryan seems to be a charming woman," Marks said with a grin. "A little garrulous, from what I've been told, but very observant."

"So I've been checked out," Julie said when she made the connection.

"Out, but not off."

"And Fran?"

Marks sighed deeply.

"What was the business about the overnight bag?"

"Look, Julie . . . Mrs. Hayes . . ."

"Julie is just fine, Lieutenant."

Marks was held up by the arrival of their waiter. He ordered a double Scotch. "Or make it Bushmill." Irish whisky.

"Much better," the waiter said.

Julie ordered a vodka and tonic.

"I'll answer your question, Julie. Then I'd like some answers from you. The inspector wanted to keep the two women apart until a few things were in place. Discrepancies are important. Mrs. Alexander agreed to go to a hotel. But I think when her lawyer got there he persuaded her to return home."

"Why?"

"I wasn't party to their conversation," Marks said with an edge, "but my guess is he wanted to force our next step. And we cooperated. We backed off. My turn now?"

Julie nodded.

"I'd like to know something about Eleanor."

"So would I," Julie said. "But I don't understand Fran going to a hotel voluntarily. Or didn't she know where she was going?"

Marks stared at her for most of a second, making it clear that he wasn't going to explain the police gambit any further. "Let's start with the attack on Alexander's picture this afternoon. What was that all about?"

"I know someone who'd call it a mighty poor sense of reality," Julie said. "With Tony already dead, why destroy the painting?"

"Does she have a history of violence?"

"She has a history of hating Tony, something she gave me a pretty willing account of this evening. But there has to be a story there that nobody's ever wanted to talk about."

Marks glanced toward the bar, impatient for his drink. "I have a feeling this is no place to be an outsider. Never mind. I have enough questions to keep us busy."

"If I don't get something to eat soon..." Julie put her hands to a very flat stomach.

"You won't want it," Marks finished her sentence. "It happens to me all too often. Was Alexander's wife really devoted to him?"

"I think so."

"Everybody says so. Enough to be dangerously jealous?"

"Sorry. I don't know how to answer that one."

"I don't blame you. What is enough?"

The waiter brought the drinks, and setting Julie's before her, said, "Weren't you in here last night—with an older woman?" He whirled his hand around over his head, describing Mrs. Ryan's bird's nest of a hat.

"Mary Ryan," Julie said.

"Ah, yes. Isn't she a character? She came back from next door with a parcel of old time actors. It was here they held the wake—till three in the morning."

Marks downed half his whisky straight and set the glass aside carefully as though what was left might last longer at a distance.

"I'm not going to bring you a menu," the waiter went on, "because we have none. Only the board and it's wiped clean at this hour. Have a nice steak."

"Rare," said Marks.

"Medium rare," Julie said. They had ordered dinner.

"You'd better drink up, sir. God knows when I'll get back to you."

"I'll drink in my own time," Marks said, "but you can bring me another."

"Cheerio, lad." The waiter was off, pulling in his white cuffs.

Julie grinned.

"If there's anything that puts me off it's a man who can see through me and doesn't hesitate to let me know it."

"You're becoming Irish," Julie said.

"I'm very susceptible to environment," Marks said with a distinct brogue. Without playing the game with himself further, he finished the whisky, and added, as he put the glass down carefully, "The policeman's friend." He lit a cigarette.

Julie turned her glass round and round, dreading to take the first sip on an empty stomach.

"What's on your mind?" Marks asked, assuming she was about to speak.

"What if I'd stayed here with Mrs. Ryan last night? Ordinarily, I might have."

"But it wasn't an ordinary night, was it? Do you have the confidence of the Alexander women?"

"I think so," she said cautiously.

"I'm not going to ask you to do anything except listen to me for now. Take Frances Alexander: was it or wasn't it strange behavior for her to wait an exact half hour for a husband who didn't show up? Then, without more than a cracker to eat, to go directly—in her evening clothes—to the dirty back room of a flower shop and start to work mixing her own concoction of potting soil, nitrogenous soil, mind you—you know what that means?"

Julie nodded. An element in gunpowder. "But, Lieutenant, about Fran's waiting a half hour for Tony: she always did that. And she didn't know he'd called. He was almost always late and they had an agreement that she'd wait a half hour only and then either eat, or go on to wherever they were going.... And maybe Fran was wearing evening clothes, but something's changed in the past few months: she doesn't care about clothes, or what her hands look like or any of those things the way she used to. I'm not surprised at her going directly to the shop.''

"All right," Marks said, "How about this? She had left the burglar alarm off purposely."

"How does Fran explain it?"

"Nobody knows it's off except herself and the daughter. She often wants to return to the shop at night—without triggering the alarm. So she simply leaves it off. As for last night, she has changed the story a couple of times—not by much, but in a way that suggests she's not telling all of the truth. She arrived at the shop in a distressed state of mind: marital troubles. Do you know about that?"

"A little," Julie said even more cautiously.

"I hope so, because my purpose is not to tell tales, but to compare information. She started to work, compulsively. Then, for some reason, she thought about the revolver and went up front to see that it was in its place. It wasn't. And because the daughter knew about the gun and had a key to the shop, Mrs. Alexander panicked. The girl has often threatened suicide. Mrs. A. called home, no answer. She called the doorman of the building. He had not seen Eleanor. So she ran all the way home. How far is it? A few blocks. And discovered a note to say Eleanor had gone to a movie. She also discovered the lids to two cans of cat food. The doorman hadn't seen the girl leave because she went out the service entrance where the door automatically locked behind her, and fed the stray cats. Not for the first time. Mrs. Alexander is relieved. Or shaken. Who knows? And for a few minutes she completely forgets about the supposedly missing gun. When she remembers it she returns to the shop, finds the revolver, only it's not in its right place, and she thinks it is she herself who is losing her mind. At which point she cleans and polishes the handgun and puts it away in its usual place, covered by a chamois cloth in a drawer beneath the cash register. Naturally leaving her own prints on it, and only hers.''

"I could buy that," Julie said.

"That's approximately the way she tells it. Now for the postscript—concerning Eleanor. During the girl's interrogation, she was asked about her fingerprints on the revolver..."

"But you just said there weren't any prints except Fran's," Julie protested.

"I know, but she was asked all the same and she started to explain how she was curious when her mother left her in charge of the shop in the afternoon, and since she'd never had a gun in her hands.... At that point she realized that her mother had taken the revolver from the shop with her so that she couldn't have handled it at that time. She backed off, said it happened the day before, and then said she couldn't remember when. But she did admit handling a gun—and to making mudpies in the shop yesterday," he added with exasperation. "Lots of soil under the nails. Potting herbs to take back to college with her."

"What about Tony's gun?" Julie asked. "Were Fran's prints on that?"

"I'm sure. Even if we can't raise them."

Julie finally took a sip of her drink.

"You'd be a cheap date," Marks said.

"I eat a lot. What else about Eleanor?"

"I asked you, remember?"

"She thinks she's a suspect," Julie said.

"She is. There's something she's not telling us either. But we'll get to it. That's where you could help." He held up his hand as Julie was about to protest. "Not as an informant. As a persuader. If she thinks we don't believe her, and she keeps saying that, encourage her to lay it all out. It's our job to understand the incredible."

"The business of nobody believing her goes back to her childhood," Julie said. "I'll see what I can do. I know some pretty decent cops and I'll tell her that."

"Thank you!" Marks laughed at the modest compliment.

"I hope it doesn't close her up even tighter."

"If it does we'll shake her loose—the hard way. The inspector is a bulldog."

As the waiter approached with Marks' second drink, Julie thought back to Mrs. Ryan and her triumphant cry on providing information Julie hadn't known: "Then I've earned my supper!" She wondered if she had earned hers.

Marks took a long pull at his cigarette and then put it out. "Do you know an actress named Patti Royce?"

Julie's heart gave a leap. "I've heard of her."

"She's in a new picture called *Celebration*. It was screened for Alexander before he went on to the mayor's party."

"A special screening?"

"So it would seem."

"I wonder if Jay Phillips was supposed to do the publicity," Julie said after a moment's thought.

Marks sighed. "Phillips again."

"I don't know that he was. It just went through my mind. Who are the producers?"

"A company called Venture Films."

"I never heard of them, but that doesn't mean anything."

"And Patti Royce: you *have* heard of her."

"She's in a new soap opera—a one-time child star making a comeback. I tried to get an interview with her last Thursday, but I couldn't get past her agent."

"On assignment from Alexander?"

"On my own initiative."

"Mere coincidence?" Talk about a bulldog.

"It seemed like a good item for the column." At least part of the truth.

"Did you discuss it with the boss?"

"No, sir."

"Any particular reason you didn't?"

"I didn't get a chance. Besides, that's not how we worked. If Tim or I got hold of something useful, we'd research it, write it up, turn it in and pray."

"I see," Marks said. "But if you didn't get a chance to talk with the boss, doesn't that mean that the idea was a recent one? In other words, Miss Royce had only, within a day or so, shall we say, come to your attention. Or am I wrong?"

Part bulldog, part fox.

"I met an actress who'd played her mother in a Broadway play ten years ago," Julie said. "Jay Phillips was the press agent. During the run his wife committed suicide. She jumped from the building where Patti Royce lived."

"I see," Marks said. "You were working the Phillips connection."

"That's right."

"Not knowing of the possibility of an Alexander connection?"

"With Patti Royce? Is there one?"

Marks looked at her wistfully over the top of his glass and then drank down the whisky. "I was hoping you'd tell me."

SEVENTEEN

SLEEP SIMPLY would not come. The day's discoveries—or deceptions—kept repeating themselves in her tired mind, changing in juxtaposition but refusing to go away. She turned over onto her back and stared at the ceiling: charcoal grey in the middle of the night. On the therapist's couch she'd had a terrible time getting into associations. Now she couldn't turn them off.

She lit the lamp beside the phone. When her eyes became accustomed to the light she dialed Mary Ryan, who was always saying to phone her at any hour.

"I THOUGHT MAYBE you'd called me today while I was out with the dog. He's such a burden, poor thing, but he won't use the papers. He must be the only dog in New York who won't go on the *Daily* in an emergency. How are you, dear? I've been thinking about you all day. What are you doing up at this hour?"

"I can't sleep. Too much has happened."

"It's terrible about your Mr. Alexander. You wouldn't have wanted that to happen to him, no matter what."

"I certainly wouldn't," Julie said.

"That's what I told the two detectives who came by to check your alibi."

"What did you tell them?"

"Nothing they didn't ask, you may be sure. I said I wasn't a bit surprised at you walking alone in the rain at night, but you know, Julie, and you coming down with a cold..."

"I'm fine," Julie said.

"What I wanted to tell you, I went to the Phillips funeral after all, and I met your Mr. Butts. He's a born-again Christian, so I don't think he could be Irish though you never know nowadays what they're into. What a fiery little man!"

"Is he a family friend or what?"

"More a business associate of Mr. Phillips', I think. He's too exotic a bird for the sisters. He used to be part owner of a circus and travelled the world with it. We had grand talk, him and me, when we went back to the house after the service—we didn't go to the cemetery—about the old days when people took responsibility for their own selves. When bootstraps were in fashion. Isn't that a lovely turn of phrase, *When bootstraps were in fashion*?"

"Very colorful," Julie said. "What else did you talk about? Did he mention Tony?"

"We talked about you."

"Oh, great."

"He felt you thought he was exploiting the contestants. You know, in the marathon dance? As though they'd enter it if they had anything better to do. What worries him is if drugs get into the picture: it's part of the physical examination now to look for needle marks. Isn't that horrible?"

Julie agreed. "Nothing about Tony?"

"I didn't say nothing. He said his death was a terrible personal loss to him. He'd been counting on his support."

"What kind of support?"

"It was my impression he meant moral support, both of them being do-it-yourself sorts. But I couldn't very well ask, could I?"

"What came up about Jay?" Who, according to Councilman McCord had co-signed eighty thousand dollars' worth of notes for Butts. Speaking of moral support.

"It was my impression, Julie, that Mr. Phillips was deeply in his debt. I got that mostly from the attitude of the sisters. They don't like Mr. Butts, but they were kow-towing to him all the same. They turned very chilly toward me when they came back from the cemetery and saw the two of us together."

Yet the sisters had arranged with McCord to take Butts to the mayor's party. He must have told them of their brother's promise. And did they know of the co-signed notes? Eighty

thousand dollars out of Jay's estate if Butts went bust. As
for the promotor's going back to Tony's office with him
after the party, why hadn't he told Mrs. Ryan about that?
"When did he line up all this moral support from Tony—did
he tell you?"

"I don't think he said. I got the impression they were
buddies, but he's like that, you know. He's pals with everybody, especially the big shots to hear him tell it. But we
know lots like him in show business now, don't we?"

Julie agreed.

"The nicest thing about the whole day when you put it all
together was Father Doyle's sermon. You felt he was talking about a human being, not just reciting something out of
a book. It made me proud to be in his parish."

"Father Doyle from St. Malachy's?"

"The same. After all, it's the Catholic actors' church and
in the theater district."

"Of course," Julie said, and her tired mind began turning over approaches to the priest on the life and death of Jay
Phillips. She heard a stifled yawn at the other end of the
line. "Go back to sleep, Mrs. Ryan. It was great to be able
to talk to you."

"Any time, dear, but I'd better hang up before you-know-
who wakes up and wants to go for a you-know-what."

EIGHTEEN

THE PRIEST made a soft clucking sound when the infant screeched at the splash of water on its little bald head. He gave it back to its mother and continued the baptismal prayers while she tried to muffle the protest. The cries subsided, but from where Julie sat at the back of the church she couldn't hear the prayers anyway.

An altar boy took away the basin and Father Doyle came down the aisle with the family, a freckle-faced Irish lot, and as happy as from a wedding ceremony. The child, now in the state of God's grace, was safe from the devil until he could do battle for himself. Julie wished she had such faith. And then there were times when she feared she might succumb to it falsely by the mere wish. She went to the steps and watched the priest where he waited with the family until one of the men in the party brought the car—a Chevrolet of age and dignity, as pristine as the flowing white baptismal gown, the train of which Father Doyle tucked in before he closed the car door. He took Julie's hand when she went to meet him. His face was rounder and puffier than when she had last seen him, his hair thinner, and beneath the vestments his greening black cuffs were shinier. "I certainly do remember you, though I might not get the name right away. You were going to choose something for me to read by William Butler Yeats. You see, I remember his name at least," he added slyly.

Julie identified herself. Then: "My friend, Mary Ryan, said you preached a beautiful sermon yesterday at Jay Phillips' funeral, and I wanted to ask you about him."

The priest sighed. "Mary Ryan is a great talker, isn't she? All right, come back to the sacristy with me while I put away the vestments, thought I don't know what I can tell you about the man."

"You don't have many baptisms in St. Malachy's, do you?" Julie said, not wanting to leap into a subject about which he seemed reluctant.

"Not as many as we used to. But you'd be surprised."

They went past the entrance to what had once been the Actor's Chapel in the church basement; it was now a seniors' center. Closed: Sunday. "We'd have a hard time without the center," the priest went on, "though what'll happen now with the government tightening our belts for us, I'm not sure."

"I remember Mrs. Ryan was outraged when the center opened, taking over the chapel for a lot of old fogies."

"She's still outraged—except when she wants a warm meal cheap and a few scraps from the kitchen for that corpulent canine of hers. There's no snobbery like that of the poor toward one another."

In the sacristy he removed the stole from over his shoulders, touched it to his lips and laid it away in a long drawer. Julie asked him the name of the white, see-through vestment, hip length, that he lifted over his head: a surplice. He took her through to the rectory, to the same tiny square parlor they had sat in once before. The only change was two new popes on the wall. "If I wrote down my sermons I'd give you a copy, for the best things I knew about the man were in it. But I say a prayer and think about the departed, and the family sitting out there, wanting to hear the best, feeling guilty themselves about the worst, needing what consolation I can give them. Then I take off, and most of what comes out fits in. It's not as though I was writing for a newspaper. Accuracy is not a requisite, thank God."

"I'd like to do something on him in our *New York Daily* column," Julie said carefully.

The priest looked at her a little sadly. "Why don't you let him rest in peace?"

"I wasn't thinking of writing anything that would disturb him, Father Doyle."

"A figure of speech. Anyone who takes his own life goes to an uneasy grave."

"I wouldn't want to distress the Phillips sisters either."

There was skepticism in the quick glance the priest gave her, but he nodded solemnly.

Julie felt the color in her cheeks. "Also a figure of speech."

They both smiled.

"Would you talk a little about Jay when you first knew him?" Julie asked.

"It goes back quite a few years," the priest said, "to when I married him to Ellen Duprey, an actress of sorts. That was before your time. He was a good deal older than her, and he suffered a bad case of scruples over it. She was a shy young woman."

"Hadn't she been a nun?"

"I don't think she finished her novitiate, and many a girl has gone in and come out finding herself unsuited for the discipline. That's what the novitiate is all about. But the two Phillips sisters made such a fuss about it when they found out, you'd have thought... well, I don't know what you'd have thought. They'd had this one and that one in mind for him over the years, but the plain truth was they didn't want him to marry at all. Look now, I'm talking gossip in spite of myself. You won't use it?"

"I won't," Julie said.

"All I'm saying, he expected them to be pleased, one of their own kind, you might say. And as for the girl, well, he was a nice man and the theater is a hard place to make your way alone."

"You're a nice man too, father," Julie said.

"It's one of my many temptations." He smiled broadly so that she saw that the missing back tooth had not been replaced.

"You know that she was also a suicide," Julie said.

"I do know that."

"Did you say the funeral Mass for her, too?"

"I didn't," he answered hastily, warily. Then, straightening up in his chair: "I'm not going into that, young lady, if that's where you're trying to lead me."

Which meant there was something there to be avoided, Julie thought. "I think my late employer, Tony Alexander, nosed out some scandal there and held it over Jay for the rest of his life."

"I know nothing," the priest said.

"I understand. I shouldn't have come to you with the kind of questions I want to ask. It's not scandal for its own sake that I'm after, Father Doyle—only for why Tony Alexander was murdered."

"Aren't the police any help?"

Julie had to laugh at herself. And to be honest. Her credentials were those of a gossip columnist.

"I didn't mean to put you down, now," the priest said.

"But you were right. I keep thinking of myself as some sort of crusader, and I'm not really."

"Well, if it's any consolation, some of those crusaders were pretty rough fellows and they were absolutely sure that, as the song goes, they had God on their side."

"Father Doyle, did you meet a Mr. Butts at the funeral or at the house?"

"A short, round man with a bounce to him?" Julie nodded. "I did meet him, and I know what made you think of him: he has God on his side."

"That's it," Julie said.

"He introduced himself to me on the church steps. I'm always uncomfortable when somebody compliments me on a sermon for the dead. It generally means I've left out something important."

Julie grinned, but persisted: "Had you met him before—or heard about him?"

The priest smiled happily. "I can truthfully say no to that one."

NINETEEN

JULIE TRIED TO THROW OFF the feeling of sadness the priest had left her with. Eighth Avenue wasn't the place to do it. The whores were out in their Sunday best. Missing, or otherwise occupied, was the red-headed girl who sang hymns of a Sunday as she high-hipped it along the avenue. "Holy God, we praise Thy name..." Did she pray to Mary Magdalen? Did Magdalen wind up a saint?

She passed Kevin Bourke's electrical shop, where every once in a while she visited the unfortunate man. A born victim, even or especially of himself. His temptation was boys, and since it was known on the street, a vicious band of young male prostitutes would taunt him and solicit and stand outside his shop and salute the cops as they drove slowly by, knowing damn well what the boys were about. Mr. Bourke lived at the Willoughby, and while his sin was known, so was his repentance. He was a source for awed gossip among Mrs. Ryan and her cronies, but like most of them he was in some way associated with the theater—in his case it was lighting equipment for the small amateur and semi-professional groups of the neighborhood—and therefore entitled to their protection. When the Willoughby management attempted to evict him after one of his episodic slips, Mary Ryan and friends blocked the hall until someone ran for Father Doyle to arbitrate the matter.

Something in the Bourke story reminded her of Phillips, something aside from Father Doyle's knowing them both. As soon as she reached the shop she got out her notebook and reviewed the entries about Phillips. There was his young wife's suicide—the virginal young wife, ex-nun, who threw herself from the building where Patti Royce, child star, lived; Tony had noted it in the column. Someone at the Actors Forum remembered how Jay hated backstage mothers.

Jay was fired from *Little Dorrit*, the child star of which, Abby Hill, was out for an appendectomy. Julie had her association: young boys, young girls. Could it be that Jay's problem was very young girls? And did Tony know and torment him for it? Was that the issue? And how about Butts in this context? Eighty thousand dollars of co-signed notes and big time publicity for a small time operation.

She phoned in for her messages. Several had piled up. Again she failed to make contact with Tim; Homicide had called to say that Alexander's office would be available to them by noon on Monday; the police had sealed the celebrity file, however, which relieved her of one anxiety. She called Alice Arthur to come in Monday afternoon and asked her to try to reach Tim to let him know they had the office back. She sat a moment and thought of what it was going to be like to be responsible for three columns a week. It was a lot of copy, even for two people, when you considered what might get thrown out by Control Central—Editorial and the legal department. And she was going to have to learn to use the video data terminal.

Panic.

She made herself answer every call, the last to the Alexander apartment. Eleanor had phoned twice since noon. It was she who answered.

"Julie, mother says she'll take us out to dinner if you'll come too. Please do. It's terrible waiting for something to happen—just the two of us—as though we were in a cage together."

The thought of sitting with them in a crowded restaurant shouting above the din—or in a quiet restaurant whispering lest they be overheard—was too much. "How about this? Come down to our apartment on Sixteenth Street—Fran knows—and I'll have my Greek friend, Gus, deliver his specialty of the day? Ask Fran if that's okay."

It was okay.

Julie sat at her desk and closed her eyes. Her old mantra came to mind from the days of meditation: it was a sound from the sea, the sibilant sound of the waves when they had spent themselves on the shore and slowly crawled back to their source. She listened for it in her mind's ear, and with its gradual coming came serenity.

It was shattered by a sharp rat-tat-tat at the door. She went to the front window and looked out through a sliver of space between the drapes. There, his umbrella poised for another assault on the door, was Morton Butts. Julie took her time going to the door. If he'd come to her he wanted something, but that in turn should tell her something.

"You do remember me, Mrs. Hayes...Morton Butts?" His smile was quick and tentative as she opened the door. "I hope you don't mind that I dropped in this way. It took some coaxing to get your address out of Mrs. Ryan."

Julie stifled the impulse to say that Mrs. Ryan also had her phone number, and invited him in. Only as far as the outer room, however, offering one of the two chairs where the only lamp shone between them. He sat forward with the umbrella between his knees. He kept his top coat on, the collar turned up.

"May I offer my sympathy on the death of Mr. Alexander?"

Julie thanked him and waited. A fiery little man, whom Mrs. Ryan had taken to despite the born-again Christian handicap. Why? And why did she herself so dislike him? It wasn't her usual way.

"I could be the last person who saw him alive. Except one, that is."

"Really," Julie murmured.

Butts blinked his eyes. "How have I offended you, Mrs. Hayes?"

"You haven't. I got into trouble with Tony over my piece on the dance marathon, and I still don't understand why."

"It's not your thing, that's all," he suggested, cheerful the instant she bent forward. "I can tell you, he didn't think you did me justice. I didn't think so myself. So, what occurred to me, why don't you and I go over the story together?"

"Did Tony give you the copy?"

"No, he didn't." Mr. Butts' nose gave a little twitch. "Isn't it in the office?"

"Not that I know of."

"It was right on his desk when I left. The police could have it, don't you think? I don't like to think of it floating into the hands of an evil-doer. You made some very strong innuendos in the last part of it."

"It was meant for Tony only. I wasn't suggesting that we go public with it in that form." What she still couldn't imagine were the circumstances under which Tony would have shown him the piece in the first place. Unless to challenge him on the property deal? Or had Tony got hold of Phillips' financial support of the little entrepreneur? As Alice said of Tony, he always looked for self-serving behind the act of charity. But Phillips was dead by then. Of only one thing was Julie certain: Tony would not have spent forty minutes on nostalgia.

"I'd like to explain how I came by the Garden of Roses if you're thinking of re-doing the piece," Butts said.

"How did you know the column was going to continue?"

"I called the city desk. There's no grass growing between my toes, Mrs. Hayes. But I ran up against something in the contestants I hadn't prepared myself for."

"Drugs," Julie said.

"That's it. I wondered, you living in this community, it didn't strike you in the first place. But Mr. A. said you could walk through hell without getting even a hotfoot."

So, Julie thought, if Tony had filed a card on her that's how it would have read—another of his spiritual types. She supposed she'd known it all along, but it was depressing nonetheless.

"I admire that, you know," Butts said, reading her like a printout. "In any case, I'm going to offer any of the dance registrants who have a drug problem an incentive to admit it, to kick the habit and start their rehabilitation right then and there during the marathon. I'm going to put them on television to tell their story, and I'm going to find sponsors for that television show. Tony Alexander said he'd do something special for us. He thought he might do some of the interviewing on the air."

"Interesting," Julie murmured. Again she was trying to see Tony as Butts described him. She knew for a fact that Tony did not like the image he projected on television: he'd tried it several times and wound up growling that he came across like a nursing home Gene Shalit. And it was crazy that Jay Phillips, who certainly knew the New York scene, would not have anticipated the drug problem in the first place. "What comes after the dance marathon, Mr. Butts?"

"Ah, that is the question, isn't it? What a smart girl you are! I think the marathon is going to catch on all over the country and maybe we can tie in everywhere the idea of dancing away the drug habit. I'd like to do it on the basis of good old-fashioned patriotism, do-it-yourself, America! I know you think I talk in clichés and I do. Clichés are the only truths I know."

"All right," Julie said. Mr. Butts was beginning to get to her. And maybe he got to Tony, who had a strong conservative streak right down his middle.

"Would you be willing to do some of the interviewing for us on the T.V.? I understand you have a theatrical background. I like your voice and I like that nice open face of yours. I don't think we'd agree on everything, but...what's the matter?"

Julie was shaking her head. "My theatrical background consists of a couple of years training as an actress, but no experience whatever. Thank you, but no, I'm going to have all I can handle to carry my half of the column. But if my partner agrees we'll try to give your rehabilitation program as much coverage as we can. Okay?"

"Who am I to say okay or nokay? Every little bit helps."

"Did Tony ask you about your future events?"

"He was interested. I would say that."

"He kept you there for a long time—for Tony."

"I think you've hit the nail on the head, Mrs. Hayes. He kept me there for Tony. I've told the police and I'll tell you: he was waiting for someone. Didn't say so, but every time I'd get to my feet, he'd insist that I tell him more about the Garden and its 'happening,' as he called it. As soon as we got to his office he'd called someone to get in touch with his wife and say he'd be an hour late. I don't flatter myself, Mrs. Hayes, that he intended to spend all that time with me. The phone rang twice with no one speaking. That upset him. Then the call to which he said, 'I'll be here.' I had an engagement myself and I finally got away. You can imagine how I feel now: If I'd stayed, would he still be alive? Or would I also be dead?''

"I've asked myself a couple of what-if questions, too," Julie said. She had begun to believe the little man. "Do you think Tony and Jay Phillips were ever friends?"

"Outside their professional association? I doubt it."

"How about enemies?'

"Why do you ask?"

"Because I saw Jay a few hours before his suicide and he referred to Tony as an s.o.b."

"Did you know Jay was dead when you came to see me?"

"Yes."

"You could have told me," he said in mournful reproach. His credibility slipped.

"I had no idea of any association between you. I didn't know he was doing your publicity. I suppose Tony did."

"Oh, yes."

"Who's going to handle it now that Jay's gone?"

"Mrs. Hayes, what do you think I'm doing here on a gloomy Sunday afternoon?"

She offered him a cup of tea and took him into the back room. He told her essentially the same story about the Garden of Roses as she'd heard from Councilman McCord and from Romano.

"How did you connect with Jay?" she asked in as casual a tone as possible.

"Oh, a long time ago. Before I turned teetotaller. Know what that means?"

"I can figure it out."

"Jay wasn't always an important Broadway publicist, and since you're checking my credentials, Mrs. Hayes, I better tell you, those Phillips sisters don't much cotton to me, and I never figured out if it was because I quit drinking or because Jay didn't."

Julie waited until they were having tea to ask, "Mr. Butts, why do you think Jay committed suicide?"

"Despair. And it's the one unpardonable sin."

"Despair over what?"

"I am my brother's keeper. Never in my life have I shirked that duty. But the grave is silent, and he chose the grave. I am also keeper of the silence."

Divine hyperbole which translated to: Mind your own business. But he knew all the same, Julie thought. If Jay Phillips' problem was very young girls, Butts knew it. Had he used it? And now why had he come to her? Several reasons surfaced, but the real one, she suspected, was still buried under the rhetoric.

When he left she went to her notebook and wrote down their conversation as she remembered it. She thought about the Phillips sisters and whether they would talk to her about him. Or about their late sister-in-law. The trouble with little old ladies like the Phillips sisters was that they often told things the way they wanted them to be or to have been. And they tended to contradict one another. Doctor Callahan had used to say she learned more about her patients from the lies they told than from the truth. Julie had never managed to ask her how she knew the difference.

TWENTY

SHE WAS BEGINNING to feel the strain of confrontation. She needed to be alone or with someone with whom she could relax. But who was that? It certainly wasn't Fran and Eleanor. On her way home, she even found her friend Gus snappish when she stopped at his restaurant. "What do you think, you get fast food by Gus? Fast food is shit. Here you get good, healthy Greek food. But you want to take out. In a half hour it's dead."

"I'll have the oven on and pop it in."

"So it dries out."

"Okay, Gus. Forget it. We'll eat Chinese."

"You will not. Monosodium glutamate. I tell you what: I give you three skewers—lamb kabobs, onion, pepper, whatever I got, everything set: all you got to do is put under the broiler. Tomorrow you bring back the skewers. You got rice? I'll give you. A little saffron?" He waved his hand in disgust. "I'll give you."

"How about dessert?"

He looked over the supply under glass on the counter. So did Julie. Most of the flies were outside the glass. "Take the *Koulourakia*. It already has bicarbonate of soda in the recipe." Gus grinned. He was enjoying himself. "You got Greek coffee?"

Jeff always bought a variety of coffees at a shop on Ninth Street. "Turkish," Julie said.

"Same thing. Goddamn Turks."

THE FRAGRANCE of Gus' marinade and saffron filled the tiny kitchen. Whatever fragrance there had been to the little cakes had been lost in a week-end under glass. Or to the bicarbonate of soda. Julie set a simple table in the combined dining room and library. She washed and changed, opened the living room doors and had a good half hour of meditation. Much refreshed, she watched at the window for the arrival of mother and daughter.

Eleanor paid the cab driver. Fran came up the steps slowly, her hand on the rail. She looked like the neighbors' cleaning lady at the end of her day's work. The stoop of her back, her step, her indifference to what was happening behind her: she looked burdened. Julie thought of the person she had known in her own early days of marriage, the wife of her husband's friend who had made her comfortable in an older, sophisticated environment. She went through the house, pressed the lock release and waited in the hall.

Fran took a long look around her, entering the downstairs hallway, as though she too was remembering, and on the way up she paused to call Eleanor's attention to the staircase. It rose in narrow grace from the vestibule to the third floor of the early nineteenth-century house. Miraculously, the vases and sculptures had not vanished from the wall cubicles, the architectural purpose of which was to facilitate the passage of furniture up the staircase. "I'd almost forgotten how beautiful it was," she said to Julie on the top step.

Julie hugged her. Again she noticed the slightly stale smell to this once elegant woman.

"I've often wondered why we don't see each other," Julie said.

"And now you know?" said with a kind of wryness.

Julie didn't answer, greeting Eleanor instead.

"Who wants what to drink?" she asked as they gave her their coats to put in the closet.

Dinner did not go badly. The talk was of Julie when Fran first met her. Julie asked questions about Jeff's former wife, which once would have been an exercise in masochism, and maybe still was. She wasn't sure of her purpose except that it connected with Eleanor.

"Talk about shy," Julie said to the girl, "I was worse than you are. Like Jeff was Maxim de Winter and I didn't even have a name."

"Rebecca," Fran explained to her daughter. "Didn't you ever read it?"

Eleanor hadn't, which left the comparison without much point.

"Actually I never read it either," Julie said, "but I saw the movie."

"I don't go to movies," Eleanor said. Then after a few seconds of acute silence, "Except *Stevie*. I've seen that five times."

Julie marked the apparent guilelessness of the girl, for she was reminded of how the police had trapped her into admitting she had handled one of the revolvers. The pattern here was the same: what appeared to be a tardy attempt at self-protection.

"Isn't it amazing," Fran said. "I think she's gone to see it every day since she's been home."

"Everybody knows me there. The cashier, the ticket man, and the manager."

"How come you went to see it in the first place?" Julie asked.

"My roommate has a crush on Glenda Jackson and she made me go with her."

"It sounds so childish," Fran said.

"I have a crush on Mona Washburn, who plays the aunt, and she must be seventy or eighty."

"My God," Fran said.

Julie said, "I can understand it."

"I suppose it's my fault," Fran said, but with a curious tone of detachment or resignation.

"If it's anybody's fault, it's Tony's."

"I thought we agreed before we left the house," Fran said.

"I simply stated a fact."

"Please, child."

"When I was a child I wasn't allowed to be one. Now you call me a child and say the things I do are childish."

"Eleanor, have I ever criticized your life-style?"

"You don't even know my life-style."

Fran, sitting hunched at the table, put her hand to her forehead. Again Julie observed the condition of her hands. The nails had been scooped out, but the grime of the shop was ground into the skin. No wearer of gloves, she.

"I like being gay," Eleanor said after a moment. "That doesn't mean I hate men. Only some men."

"Must you go on like this?"

"Yes. I want to be understood at least by Julie."

Julie realized she had suspected the gay part.

Fran drew a long, deep breath. Then: "Violence makes us the more violable. Nothing is sacred. Nothing is private." She looked at Julie after a glance at her daughter. "We are terrible living with one another just now, and you would think we might find consolation in one another's company."

"You would think it, wouldn't you, now that he's dead?" Eleanor said to Julie.

"Really, we should go," Fran said, "and not embarrass Julie like this."

"Are you embarrassed?" Eleanor pounced. There were dabs of color high in her cheeks and the vein was inevitably prominent. Over Julie's demur, she carried on her attack on her mother. "It isn't as though I couldn't understand how hurt she was. All my life I've been wildly, humiliatingly jealous. Helpless because of it."

"Poor child," Fran said.

"Oh, mother, take off."

Fran had it coming, Julie felt. She said, "The jealous *are* helpless—as long as they hang in. I want to ask both of you something: have you been able to talk with one another about Tony's death?"

"I cannot, and she won't stop," Fran said.

"That's not true. I wish I never had to hear his name again in all my life."

They hadn't been able to talk, and it wasn't going to happen now, not on this tack. Nor could Julie get her fork into the dessert. "These little cakes are pretty awful, aren't they?"

"They're like hockey pucks," Eleanor said: the perfect image.

Fran said, "But the rest of the dinner was delicious. And the wine."

"Jeff's selection," Julie murmured.

Fran raised her glass and hesitated an instant before drinking. "They were such good friends," she said.

Eleanor interpreted to her own bitter taste. "Are you going to break the glass now, mother?"

"You're being tiresome."

Julie put her hand on Eleanor's and said, "Look, chum, it was only last night that you told me how much you loved your mother. If you want me to understand, you'd better clarify the issue."

"Mother knows what a liar I am." She stabbed at the little cake and it skittered off her plate and onto the floor. She got the giggles.

Julie moved away from the table. "How about walking down to the Village and having ice cream?"

GREENWICH VILLAGE was in its Sunday night lull, which meant that the tourists had given it back to the natives. "Most of the week-end," Julie said, "you can't see the poets for the cowboys. If you can see through the pot smoke in the first place." That reminded her: "Fran, have you ever heard of someone named Morton Butts?"

"Not that I remember. Except for the police asking it also. An odd name. I think I'd remember it."

"You don't approve of pot?" Eleanor wanted to know.

"Let's say I don't like it. No, let's say I don't approve of it. If it was legal maybe I'd have to rethink it."

"You're funny," Eleanor said.

"What about Morton Butts?" Fran asked.

"I wrote an article about him and the dance marathon that Tony hated."

"Tony was in one once, you know."

"Mmmm. Varicose veins."

"He was so vain," Fran said forlornly.

Eleanor made a noise of distaste and dropped behind to look in a shop window.

"This Butts went back to the office with Tony from the mayor's party. He stayed till nine thirty. Would they talk about a dance marathon all that time?"

"Julie, please don't put me through a police-like inquisition. They have already done it rather thoroughly."

"Sorry," Julie said.

"You don't need to be sorry."

Just shut up, Julie told herself, but she couldn't. "It's important that the police find out why Tony went back there, Fran."

"Then let them find it out. I will not participate further."

"Then you already know," Julie said. "Or think you know and don't want to face it. Don't you want to know who killed him?"

Fran stopped abruptly and let the people close behind them pass on. "Will that bring him back?" she asked, and turned back to where Eleanor had gone into the store. Julie had no choice but to follow her. They waited at the window. Leather goods and Indian beads. Eleanor was deciding on a string of beads.

"For her roommate no doubt," Fran said. "She adores her."

"An older person?"

"She'll be looking for a mother all her life."

"Or a grandmother," Julie said.

"I have tried to love her," Fran said. "Isn't that a cruel thing for a mother to have to say?"

Julie nodded, watching Fran's eyes reflected in the store window. Anger started in them.

"She simply would not allow me to—as long as there was Tony. And now…" Fran shook her head vehemently. "And now, as though his death were not enough, she would destroy even his picture on the wall.... And she told you how much she loved me?"

"She did," Julie said. "Except when you won't let her."

"When I won't let her," Fran said. "I suppose we're both right about it. And both wrong."

BACK IN THE APARTMENT they managed small talk about Greenwich Village while Julie served the thick, sweet coffee. Then Fran remarked, "Tony used to say it was the last playground of a man's youth."

Eleanor exploded. "How can you remember something like that now? I don't understand you, mother."

"Nor I you," Fran said.

"Mother, Tony's new girlfriend isn't any older than me, and that's disgusting."

"He was infatuated, that's all."

"He wanted a divorce," the girl shouted.

"He only thought he wanted one. He was at an age when it was important to him that women found him attractive."

"Stop defending him!"

"Until I die."

"When will you go back to school, Eleanor?" Julie asked clumsily.

"As soon as the police say I can." She took hold of her mother's wrist. "I'm going to tell you something I've been hiding for years, trying to forget..."

Fran groaned.

"If you listen to me, mother, maybe you'll understand if Julie does."

Imperfect logic, and yet...

Fran bowed her head and settled her eyes on the strong hand wrapped around her wrist. The girl's knuckles had gone white.

"When I was eleven years old and came here on a visit, Tony promised me a great treat one day when you were at the shop. He took me downtown to meet someone he said was important in the theater, and I remember him combing my hair for me and pinching my cheeks to bring more color into them. We were backstage in an empty theater, then waiting in a dressing room and I was looking at myself in the mirror. I pretended it was my dressing room. I was pretty. It's true. I've turned into a pony or something with a long face, but I *was* pretty and foolish. I won't say I was innocent. I can't remember ever being innocent..."

Fran closed her eyes. Julie was stiff with a sudden tension.

"Then this man came and asked me if I wanted to be an actress when I grew up and of course I said I did. Tony went out and left us...I didn't know where he went, but I wasn't scared at first. The man seemed very nice..." She paused and swallowed a mouthful of saliva.

"You don't need to go on," Fran said.

"I do need to because I want Julie to tell me if she thinks I could make up a story like this." She wiped her mouth on the back of her hand. "He said I was a little Joan of Arc. He was so gentle. Even now I remember the way he put his hands on my shoulders and had me kneel down in front of him. At first I thought he was praying, then he lifted my face and there were tears running down his...and then, and then when he was trying to get me to do what he wanted, Tony crashed open the door. He'd been waiting outside all the time, knowing what was going to happen."

Fran shook her head.

"Yes, mother, yes!"

"How in the name of God could he have known?"

"But he did. The man said so to him. And to this day, do you know what I remember most, what's burned into my mind? Shame. As though it had all been my fault, and what I'll remember until I die is the smug, superior look on Tony when he came in the room and hit the man in the face and then in the stomach and then in the groin, and the man just stood there and took it, his arms hanging down straight. 'I know, I know,' he kept saying. And do you know what Tony said afterwards to me when we were out on the street? He said, 'If you don't tell your mother, I won't.'" At last Eleanor fell silent.

Fran lifted her head. "But he did tell me. He was beside himself that he'd left you alone with such a person, and it was sheer accident that he'd gone back. He was supposed to be interviewing someone in the theater lounge where the cameras had been set up. We talked about it all night—

whether we shouldn't both talk to you. But Tony had given the man a beating in front of you and we decided that further discussion would only prolong the trauma. You'd heard and seen enough to know that it was wicked, and if anything like it ever happened again you would know to run, to scream."

"I have been running," Eleanor said. "Oh, yes. I have been running." She spoke directly to Julie: "I know it isn't so, but I've always thought that in spite of everything, she needed me."

Julie prayed, almost aloud: Fran, say she's right.

But Fran was silent. She rubbed her wrist where Eleanor had finally let go of it.

Eleanor said, "Damn you, mother. Damn you, damn you, damn you!"

TWENTY-ONE

THE FIRST THING Julie did Monday morning was recheck the date of *Autumn Tears*. It jibed with Eleanor's story, so that almost certainly Tony had taken her to the Irving Theater where *Tears* was playing, Patti Royce the star, Jay Phillips the press representative. But no names were spoken last night by either Fran or Eleanor.

On the phone Julie managed to clear up one thing: Jay Phillips had *not* been working on publicity for the soon-to-be-released Patti Royce picture, *Celebration*. His office had never heard of it. One tiny knot untied.

She locked up the shop and walked a few blocks north to precinct headquarters where she got to see Detective Russo, an acquaintance who was the warmer toward her because his wife and Mrs. Ryan were chums. Russo, second generation Italian-American, had grown up in the neighborhood. His parents still ran a fruit shop at Ninth Avenue and Thirty-ninth Street. He took her upstairs to the interrogation room where they shared the long table with a couple of offenders and the officers who had brought them in.

"The hospitality of the house," Russo said. "We're redecorating the living room. What can I do for you?"

"Information about child molestation," Julie said. "It is a criminal act, isn't it?"

"The first offense is a misdemeanor in New York State. I think I have this right. After that it's a felony. But it's sticky business. It's like rape used to be—still is in some cases—it's easy to throw doubt on the victim. The question of seduction is bound to come up, especially if the victim has reached puberty."

"And feels guilty about it herself," Julie said. "I'm speaking of girls."

"I figured. And then kids don't tell. And mothers of kids who do are often afraid that the fathers will find out and land in jail for trying to kill the perpetrator. That's how it plays in this part of town." Russo went on to cite several cases he knew about. "When you do collar a molester, nine times out of ten he gets off on the promise of psychiatric help. I don't know what else I can tell you, Julie."

"You've been very helpful."

"I'll get you a number at the desk. The best thing to do is take it up with the child abuse people. They got the savvy and these days they've got the clout."

"Thank you," Julie said. She wanted now to talk to Doctor Callahan, but it would have been less than gracious not to take the number he proposed to get for her.

As they were leaving the room, one of the prisoners called out to her, "Hey, lady. You a lawyer?"

"Sorry," Julie said.

"Man, you don't know what sorry is."

JULIE STOPPED at the Actors Forum, hoping to run into Madge Higgens who had played Patti's mother in *Autumn Tears*. The only person on hand was Reggie Bauer who spent most of his waking hours there. He might once have been the child actor he claimed, but Julie doubted he had done a day's work since his voice changed. She had heard he lived on his wit and his winnings at bridge. He greeted her with congratulations on that morning's by-line.

"Thanks."

"It's an ill wind, as my sainted grandmother used to say. You don't need a side-kick, do you, someone with a strong inclination to evil?"

"As your sainted grandmother used to say?"

"Yes, as a matter of fact. I used to sneak a midnight read of the Baltimore Catechism at her house. I thought it was pornography."

Julie thought about Reggie and Tim: they were very much alike. "Do you know anybody in the cast of *Little Dorrit*?"

"I *can* know someone. Give me twenty-four hours and tell me what you want to find out about whom. You may count on discretion and confidentiality. Pay is optional. Take a chance on me, huh?"

"All right. Abby Hill went out of the show with appendicitis last week. I'd like to know when the attack came on and where she's hospitalized, if she still is."

"She's English," Reggie said. "Probably went home to have the operation on the health plan. Hound dog Bauer is on the scent. I'm kidding about her going home."

"You may be right."

Reggie grinned. "What you really want to know is whether the affliction from which she suffered was actually appendicitis. Right?"

"You said it, I didn't," Julie said blandly.

SHE STOPPED AT THE SHOP long enough to phone her former therapist between patients. She asked for a one-shot although she didn't put it that way.

"Is it a crisis?" Doctor Callahan wanted to know.

"No. It's just that I need more insight than I have."

"Who doesn't?" the doctor said and gave her an afternoon cancellation.

TWENTY-TWO

ALICE ARTHUR and a man from the custodial department were rearranging the office when Julie arrived. The big room smelled of fresh paint. A transparent tarpaulin covered the card files with a sign that read, *Do not open by order of the police*. The couch had been released. Tony's desk was gone, Julie's and Tim's partners' desk was moved to where it had stood. She studied it for a moment and then said, "Let's turn it half way around." She didn't want to sit where Tony had, and she didn't think Tim would want to either.

The man from custodial called downstairs for help, rejecting the women's offer to move it with him. Gallantry, or union regulations? He identified himself on the phone as Jasper.

Alice remarked that it was a lot of work for just two more weeks of occupancy. Julie tried to picture Alice working out of the shop on Forty-fourth Street where she was thinking of taking up her own headquarters. Most of the *Daily* columnists worked away from the newspaper's offices. What came through about Alice was that Julie didn't know her very well. Tim she knew better, knowing how and what he wrote. He had a natural talent for purveying gossip. It was compounded of such ingredients as bitchiness, drollery—and a little droolery, to coin a word: you had to treat the stars with reverence if not respect; you had to have an instinct for who was on the way up and who down, for whether cats were in, or dogs, or marmosets; and the sense to know that diamonds were not a girl's best friend when the bottom had just fallen out of the diamond market. Tim had already come and gone. He'd left a dozen items for Alice to type and hand over to Julie.

"Mr. Jasper?" Julie said when he hung up the phone on Alice's desk.

"Johnny Jasper, ma'am." He was fifty or so, an intelligent looking man. In a different uniform he'd have looked like a major at least.

"How would you go about getting into the building after hours without Security knowing?"

"Well, we've been working that over with the police since Friday night, and you'd be surprised."

Julie invited him to sit down opposite her at the conference table.

"Take for example the cleanup crew: they come to the north door at nine and ring the bell. Somebody from custodial goes up and lets them in. They punch a time-clock, work nine to five, a crew of twenty up to thirty. Most of them are women, mostly black or Hispanic. They're a younger lot than in my early days around here, and there's a big turnover. Some of them know one another from outside work, but I think a stranger who knew the ropes could come in with them and then disappear without being missed. The police are working on something like that now, the boss was saying.

"And then you got the plant downstairs, remember. All that equipment takes servicing, and the trucks load up with the early editions and roll out all night and early morning. I seen your eyebrows go up at me calling down for help. Now if you want a real tough bunch of union men, you take the teamsters running the newspaper trucks. We call them 'the horses' because they run to win. Many a loader's been caught on the wrong side of the tailgate and found himself in another borough before they put him down."

"No kidding," Julie said.

"I'm exaggerating a little, but there's a lot of ways to travel all through this building if you know them. Take the elevator system, especially on the plant levels. If I was to tell you where the key was to the freight elevator, you could take it to the fourth floor and switch over to the public elevators there without seeing a soul at most hours of the day or night."

"You'd think I'd know the building myself after a year, wouldn't you?" Julie said.

"Either that or you'd know who to partner up with—if you had murder in mind."

"If I had murder in mind, I don't think I'd partner up with anybody."

"It's done all the time," Jasper said, "like it was a business deal. I tell you everything's a deal nowadays. Everybody's on the take, and they don't see anything wrong with it. You show me a man who admits he's a crook and I'll show you an honest man."

NOT ONE MAN, but three arrived from custodial. The desk was turned and nobody got a hernia.

When they had gone Alice said, "I took down what he was saying. I take down everything these days. Would you like me to type it up for you?"

"Thanks," Julie said. "You never know."

She read Tim's copy as Alice rolled it out of the typewriter: Alice was being very helpful. All of Tim's items were usable as written, none of them memorable or libelous, bits of fluff, an occasional barb. She thought of Eleanor's censorious question on the importance of interviews and previews. "Alice, have you ever met Eleanor, Tony's stepdaughter?"

"Never."

"Or heard Tony talk about her?"

"No. He used to send her a check every month until her mother took it over. Substantial too, for a school girl."

"I don't suppose she ever sent them back?"

"Ha. As Johnny Jasper said, everybody's in on the take."

A curious view of a father's allowance.

"Ever met Patti Royce?"

Alice sat an inch or two taller in her posture chair. "I will not tell tales about Tony, even if it costs me my job not to."

"I'm not asking you to tell tales. In all the years Jeff and I knew Fran and Tony—Jeff a lot longer than me—we thought of them as a great couple, the best marriage we knew. And maybe it was. Fran isn't blaming him for his divertissements or whatever you want to call them. She's even more loyal to him than you are."

"That sly little woman," Alice said with undisguised hatred.

Startled, Julie said nothing.

"She liked to see him suffer and succumb. Oh, yes. The martyr, she could live on her forgiveness of him. Tony was all man. That's not very fashionable these days. It's made fun of in sophisticated circles and called *macho*..." Alice ran on, almost out of control, her complexion a dappled pink. "Everybody thinks it was him that liked to play with guns. It wasn't. He felt he had to, but she enjoyed it. It was like gambling in her blood."

Julie listened, but more with the hope that it would soon run out than in anticipation of learning anything. If the tone and the material had been less offensive, she could have felt sorry for Alice who was casting light mostly on herself. A shame, since the locked-up part of Alice's mind had to contain both the good and the bad of Tony. Had no woman seen him from a neutral position? Yeah. Julie Hayes. Then she remembered being hurt at his non-sexual view of her.

Alice sniffed, and the vituperation began to thin out. She had to stop altogether to use a Kleenex. After a moment or two, she said, "I've blown it, haven't I? I didn't mean to talk about her. I know you're friends."

"You haven't blown anything," Julie said. "But we've got to talk about Patti Royce—if she's part of what happened to Tony. You could at least tell me as much as you told the police."

"What I told them was supposed to be confidential."

"Nothing you tell them or me is going to hurt Tony now."

"Won't help him either, will it?" Alice said and blew her nose again. Fran had said the same thing. "I told the police she was somebody he saw regularly. He'd helped her get a job in this film, *Celebration*. I said I didn't know if they were lovers, and I don't."

"Do you remember when it started between them?"

"I think the first I knew about it was when he was helping her with the part. It was about a retarded girl. I came across some pages of the screenplay—in the back of the sofa where they'd slipped down behind the cushions.''

"Who sent him the script? Do you know?"

Alice shook her head. "I never even saw it or heard about it till it was in production. Tony called it a sleeper when he talked about it, 'our little sleeper.' And believe it or not, Julie, I used to hear him mention P.R. on the telephone—once even to your husband, if I'm not mistaken—and I thought he was talking about public relations. Then I caught on, and all of a sudden things seemed to come together."

The reference to Jeff wasn't lost on Julie, but she pressed Alice to remember: "What kind of things?"

"Well, him making an appointment with his lawyer and saying something like, 'You know what I'm talking about,' in other words not wanting to talk in front of me. And he would make dates to meet people here when I wasn't going to be in the office."

"With whom besides P.R.?"

"I just don't know. They never went into his regular appointment book."

"Could I see the appointment book?" Julie asked.

"When Lieutenant Marks returns it."

Nothing came easy. "How about the screening of *Celebration* on Friday: was that in the book?"

"Only the address I jotted down. Miss P.R. herself called while Tony was at his gun club. 'Tell him we're screening the picture at the Eleven Hundred at five o'clock this afternoon. Tell him I'll be there. This is Patti Royce speaking.' Right out in the open. And I swear the way she said it, she'd been practicing in front of the mirror. Practicing to be a star."

"She was a star once," Julie said. "A child star."

"She sounds as though she's practicing to be a child too."

"Keep that up and you'll get a by-line," Julie said. "When did you give Tony the message?"

"After Mrs. Alexander had left."

"Also after you'd reserved the table for them at the Samovar?"

"Yes."

"It makes you wonder," Julie said, "if whatever delayed him in his date with Fran wasn't set up at the screening."

TWENTY-THREE

SHE WENT DOWNSTAIRS to see the editor of the Sunday magazine section, Ray Duggan. When she started to introduce herself, Duggan waved her down. "I know who you are," he said. He was what was left of an old-fashioned newspaperman: a palsied hand, a strong lead paragraph, and a preference for language over jargon.

"Any chance of selling you a story on the comeback of a child star?"

"How far back has she come, and how well-known was she compared, say, to Shirley Temple?"

"She did a couple of plays and a movie that wasn't great. But now she has a lot going for her."

"Such as?"

"A daytime television series and a new movie called *Celebration*."

Duggan ran his hand through his thinning hair, parting it in five places. "What's her name?"

"Patti Royce."

"I remember her. The play was *Autumn Tears*, am I right? She seduced the man who was driving the other car in an accident. From her wheel chair, which looked more like a perambulator." Duggan made a face. "A terrible play. The movie was even worse. Sorry, Julie, but I must be one in a hundred thousand who'd remember her."

Julie took a deep breath. "It's bound to come out soon that she was romantically involved with Tony Alexander at the time of his death."

Duggan looked at her mournfully. "Girl, when are you going to learn to put your lead in the first paragraph?"

Duggan's assignment gave her "Feature" status for which she felt the need in order to get through to Patti Royce. She went next to the advertisement department to see if space had been bought for *Celebration*. A one-eighth page ad was scheduled for the following Sunday, the ad already made up. Julie got a copy of the proof and took it upstairs with her.

While she studied it, Alice looked over her shoulder. You couldn't tell what Patti looked like from half a face—the other half had gone to black—one eye and that half-closed and half a sulky mouth. The ad was headed: *The Story of an Unforgiven Sin. Celebration* was due to open at the Spectrum on Friday—that would be a week from the following Friday.

Alice pointed to the bottom line: *This picture is unrated*.

"It looks like a 'Z' to me," Julie said.

Between incoming phone calls she read the credits to Alice. The office had come alive. *Our Beat* was making its own way.

"Ever hear of Venture Films?" Julie asked.

"I can't remember. Like somebody's name being Smith or Jones."

"How about Romulus Productions?" Listed as coproducers.

"Why don't I call the Film Board?"

"Let me try it another way first," Julie said. She called the Eleven Hundred and asked for their schedule of screenings. Among the day's showings was *Celebration* at five. Her appointment with Dr. Callahan was at three.

TWENTY-FOUR

"I'M NOT a consulting engineer," the doctor said. "I cannot say to you, add this much pressure to that much jealousy and you will reach the point of combustion."

"I understand, Doctor. But I'm not very good on mothers and daughters as you may remember, and I guess that's why I wanted to talk with you."

"You are still guessing?"

"That is the reason," Julie amended. Doctor Callahan hadn't changed much. She looked a little older and her hair was a different shade of brown, confirming the tint job Julie had always suspected, but her psychiatry was as precise as ever.

"I would rather talk about you," she said.

"I'm fine," Julie said.

"You are working?"

"In the same job for a year on the very day Jeff left for Paris. That's when all these things began to happen."

"He went to Paris again without you?"

"He often does, Doctor."

"And you are asking about jealousy? Or don't you care?"

"I sometimes wonder if there's someone, but I'd rather not know." Just like that: she had said something of which she had not been aware until in the therapist's presence.

"It is a way of coping, yes?"

Julie nodded.

"Do you make enough money to support yourself?"

"Yes, but not in the style to which I've become accustomed."

"Good. I am glad you have become accustomed to something besides pimps and prostitutes. How is your friend, the gentleman gangster?"

Julie smiled. She very nearly laughed aloud.

"What?"

"You are a Jewish mother."

She gave a great shrug. "I have children and I am Jewish. What else could I be? I am also the wife of a man named Callahan. We are in America, yes?"

"Forgive me," Julie said.

"For what? Admitting your curiosity? Let me say this about jealousy. It is a most natural thing, but like so many natural things we do, we are ashamed. And therefore we try to suppress it or to hide it. I am more fascinated by the girl than by the mother. Is it possible that she too wanted this man for herself? That from childhood she was doing tricks to make him pay attention to her? And if you are right that the mother was obsessive about him, it might explain why she kept the child away so much of the time. So now you have a lesbian—you understand, I am not talking about cause and effect—I am saying you have this girl with a devotion to an older woman. Who nevertheless comes *post haste* when her step-father says her mother needs her. Does she come for that reason or because *he* asks her to come? And when she gets here, why did he want her? So he can escape to another woman, a girl her own age, while she quarrels with the mother? These are all questions. I have no answers. I should like to know how she fantasized about him. This violation you describe, when she was eleven: It is interesting that she would say she was never innocent. But this violation, is it possible she wanted her step-father in that situation?"

"I don't think so, Doctor."

"It is far out, yes?"

Julie nodded.

"In any case, child molesters are almost always impotent."

"No kidding," Julie said.

Doctor Callahan frowned and Julie silently composed the unspoken retort for her: if you are grown-up, speak like it.

What the doctor said was: "All the same, you might be surprised if you could break into her fantasy. What is there unfinished that she chops up a dead man's portrait?"

"You don't buy the idea of her trying to draw the police's attention away from her mother?"

"I would buy that she was trying to draw attention to herself, yes. Something does not ring true: if she hated him so much, why not celebrate the divorce? Mother and daughter against the world?"

"Because her mother wasn't about to accept her in that role."

"Role," the doctor repeated almost contemptuously. "Everyone is acting, including the mother. She might not tell the daughter who her husband was involved with—but not to want to know herself? That is ridiculous. Believe me, she knows."

"But, Doctor, when *I* said I'd rather not know if Jeff had someone, you said it was a way of coping."

"I asked if it was a way of coping. Situations differ. I will not comment. Needs differ, people differ." The doctor was becoming exercised, a rare experience for Julie. "It is all fanciful, this conversation of ours. And very unprofessional of me. I would like to help you, but don't you see that I could be doing you more harm than good?"

"No. This is the environment of discovery," Julie said. "I am not taking anything literally, just trying to expand on what I do know. In the end it will be the police who decide on whether there's enough evidence to make an arrest, and the evidence will not be fanciful. It will go to things like witnesses and opportunity and a lot about those two revolvers." Julie told her then of Tony's secretary's tirade against Fran. "We've talked a lot here about jealousy, Doctor. But I keep thinking that if jealousy was the motive, Tony's killer would have wanted to get *both* him and his friend."

"His paramour?"

"His paramour." That was one Julie was not likely to have come up with on her own.

"Then she, the wife, let's say, would have surrendered to the police and would now throw herself on the mercy of the court," the doctor summarized, "and she would be acquitted: classic French justice. But in America, remember Scarsdale. Does she have a lover?"

"No, no, no," Julie said.

"It is not unheard of that women take lovers to get their husbands back."

"Does it work?"

"I am told so, but I would not look to it for a lasting cure. Why do you smile?"

"I was remembering when you used to say, 'I am not a marriage counselor.'"

"It is true. But neither do I break up marriages unless it is a last resort. There are reasons people marry one another. The reasons are much harder to change than the partner, but it is the reasons that concern me."

"Fran married Tony twenty years ago. According to Eleanor she left Eleanor's father to do it. Then he was killed. Eleanor thinks her mother had terrible guilt."

"How old was Eleanor then?"

"An infant."

"So how could she know about her mother's guilt?"

"It's a Catholic thing."

"Pah!" The sound of scorn. "That tells me nothing unless you put it in the context of the human being, a very long process. What about this Tony Alexander? He was a friend of your husband's. What does your husband say about him?"

"I don't think he's been entirely frank with me about Tony. It's funny: I didn't know until the other day that he resented my asking Tony for a job without consulting him first."

"Does that give you anxiety?"

"No."

"Good," the doctor said.

"You're right, though. I don't know enough about Tony. I don't know if he was married before. I didn't know until

Fran told me—or else I deliberately forgot—that he was Jeff's best man when he married Felicia.''

"I thought we were going to get through the hour without her name coming up."

Julie gazed across the room and said, "I wouldn't have felt I got my money's worth, Doctor."

The doctor gave a curt nod, seeming not to have found Julie's response as amusing as she had intended. She released the brake on her analyst's chair, the old signal. "I would ask you one question: why don't you leave it to the police?"

"Because I am a newspaperwoman."

"Brava! I like that answer."

Julie repressed the impulse to modify, to explain. And when she left the doctor's office, she believed it herself. It was the best session she had ever had. Lying on a couch with your toes in the air was for the birds. Dead birds.

TWENTY-FIVE

JULIE WAITED till the last minute to go upstairs to the screening room at 1100 Sixth Avenue. She slipped in, no questions asked, just before the door closed. The overhead lights were a sickly amber making the selected audience look like hepatitis victims. The scented deodorizer failed to cover the smell of stale tobacco.

Selecting the nearest seat in an empty row, Julie found herself behind a woman sitting alone in the next row, a seat away from the aisle. As soon as Julie was seated the woman, a vivid blonde, turned to speak to her.

"Good evening. I hope you enjoy the picture." Her large eyes brimmed with friendliness. Her eyebrows and lashes were dramatically dark in contrast to the blond hair. And you could tell from the inflection she had repeated the greeting many times.

Julie murmured her thanks and said she expected to enjoy it.

"My brother is one of the producers," the woman volunteered.

"Miss . . . ?"

"Mrs. Conti."

As the lights began to dim, Mrs. Conti faced forward. Then she turned and said, "Tell me later if you think the picture should be given an X-rating."

Was she for or against it, Julie wondered. The advertisement said the picture had not been rated. The viewers, perhaps fifty of them in the middle section of the theater, shared a camaraderie that suggested common employment, and Julie didn't think it was in show business. She touched the woman's shoulder. "Who's the showing for, Mrs. Conti?"

"Beauticians. People Ron invited through the Convention Bureau."

The sound was coming up, country fiddle.

"And you?" Mrs. Conti said over her shoulder in the now darkened house.

Julie said that she worked for the *New York Daily*. She wasn't sure Mrs. Conti had heard her until the woman gave a tardy and thoughtful "Huh."

A long-waisted man took the aisle seat alongside Mrs. Conti. Julie moved over a seat to better see the screen. She could also see the man better when lights came up on the screen, a hard young face with a long nose. Similar to Mrs. Conti's she noticed in their brief tête à tête.

On the screen the credits ran over a birthday cake with candles while, off-camera, three unharmonious male voices sang, "Happy Birthday." The camera pulled back to show the birthday girl, Patti Royce, who looked like a child and was so made up and costumed, very blue eyes wide with wonder, brown curls—Julie'd had a doll once with curls just like hers . . .

Cut to the men: a middle-aged, tired looking father you knew had dandruff and false teeth; the boy also with very blue eyes and straw-colored hair, the wholesome type: father, son and daughter. She had seen the actor who played the father many times; finally, among the principals there was the stranger who looked like, but wasn't, Jon Voight.

Cut to Patti, mouth puckered, cheeks puffed. Her brother moved into the frame and helped her blow out the candles. The producers' and director's credits appeared as Patti cut the cake. Close-up: Patty in deep concentration. Her tongue appeared at the corner of her mouth just for an instant, a quick pink dart. There were whistles from the audience.

The picture was good and Julie became involved. Patti Royce was a perfect twelve-year-old twenty, whose younger brother caught up with and passed her in school work, and protected her from the taunts of the kids who lived around the small-town lumber yard and called her "Dummy." The incest theme was muted and therefore stronger, and the brother's jealousy of the stranger more threatening. The bible-reading father was played by a good actor: you hated his rigidity, but at the same time he broke your heart because you knew his was breaking.

The last frames of *Celebration* showed Patti rocking a doll in a living room desolate of a woman's care while her father read aloud from the Book of Ruth. The stranger was dead, the brother was wanted for his murder. When the lights came up, most of the women in the audience were dabbing at their eyes.

Mrs. Conti turned and introduced Ron Morielli, her brother and Patti Royce's business manager. He was already on his feet and lighting a cigar. "I'm sorry," Mrs. Conti said, "I didn't get your name."

"Julie Hayes. It's a good picture, and I don't see why, Mrs. Conti, it has to be X-rated." She caught a reaction from Morielli that showed him to be less than pleased, and added, "Unless for some reason you want it released that way." She assumed that the removal of some of the brother-sister footage would upgrade the rating to R, restricted.

Morielli took the cigar from his mouth. "Are you a reviewer, Miss?"

"I want to write a feature article on Patti Royce for the Sunday Magazine."

"So you want to meet the kid?"

"I do."

"Let me introduce you before she comes out to take a bow," Morielli said. "We got her meeting fans as fast as she makes them."

Julie, already propelled toward a door beneath the projection booth by Morielli's hand at her elbow, called back that she was glad to have met Mrs. Conti.

A publicity man was talking to the audience.

Patti was sitting alone in a smallish room with easy chairs, a bar and a conference table. An ash blonde off screen, she sat, languid, a cola-colored drink in her hand, her attitude one of relaxed expectation. She wore a beige wool dress that showed a lot of cleavage.

"Hi," she said to Julie before the introductions. Throaty voice. A real, old-fashioned sex object.

When Morielli said Julie's name aloud it seemed to register with him that he had heard it before.

Julie got her pitch in fast. "I'd like to do a story on you, Miss Royce, for the Sunday Magazine of the *New York Daily*. I enjoyed *Celebration* very much."

Patti looked from Julie to Morielli and back as though she wondered how they impressed one another.

"It's a good art film besides whatever else it is," Julie added.

"That's nice," Patti said, making two syllables of the word *nice*.

"Explain to her what you mean," Morielli said.

"Ron, I know what she means. She means any jerk can understand it, only some understand more than others." Then to Julie, "Sweetie, pull one of those chairs over close and tell me what you want to say about me in the Sunday paper."

"Not now," Morielli said. "They'll want you out front in a couple of minutes.... Ma'am, why don't you send us a list of questions and take it from there?"

Patti said, "Do me a favor, Ron? Go tell them I need a few more minutes to relax." Her hand at the neckline of her dress, she gave it a scarcely noticeable tug that exposed another swatch of breast. If she were any more relaxed, Julie thought, her clothes would fall off.

He went, but after a hesitation that made him look like a character in an Edward G. Robinson movie.

"Maybe we could set a date and place," Julie said, and pulled the nearest chair a little closer to the actress. "I don't care for the idea of written questions."

"You worked for Tony, didn't you?" Patti said in a soft drawl.

"Yes."

"Is that why you want to interview me, because of Tony?"

"That has something to do with it," Julie admitted.

"I didn't bring him much luck, did I?"

"Afraid not," Julie said.

Patti glanced toward the door. "You say where we should meet. Make it in the early evening and I'll try and be there."

"You're filming in the Ninth Avenue Studios, right?"

"Almost every day." She sighed. "Life is funny." She sounded like every actress Julie had ever known on the verge of a first success: life is funny.

"How about tomorrow if you can make it?" Julie took a card from her purse. "I have an office of sorts on Forty-fourth Street. I'll pick you up in a cab at the studio entrance and we can get there in about five minutes."

Patti looked at the card and then gave it back. "You keep it. That's not far from the Actors Forum, is it?"

"Down the street."

"I adore the Actors Forum. I'd love to be a member some day."

"You will be," Julie said. She was not about to say that she was herself a member. Not to the actress she had just seen in *Celebration*.

"You're sweet," Patti said. "Pick me up at six at the side entrance on Fifty-eighth Street, and we won't tell a soul. Okay?"

"Okay," Julie said, but it seemed a mighty strange condition to put on a newspaper interview.

TWENTY-SIX

"You've GOT TO GO see it, Tim," Julie said over a beer at Downey's. They had finally caught up with one another and just had time for the corned beef and cabbage special before Tim went to a preview of *Alice the Wonder Child.*

"I'll go," Tim said. "Would you like me in on the interview?"

"No."

"I'll trade you *Alice.*"

"Be serious, Tim. We don't have much time."

"Don't say that. It sounds like prophecy. Doomsday ahead."

Julie thought of Reggie Bauer from the Forum who was looking into *Little Dorrit* for her. She told Tim about him, suggesting that he might qualify if they ever needed a legman. "He's a lot like you."

"Isn't one of me enough?" Tim said. "I know one of you would do me just fine."

Julie reached across the table and gave his hand a squeeze. It was nice noise, nothing more. "Will you find out for me all you can about the producers and maybe even the distributor?"

Tim had the *Celebration* hand-out in front of him. The only art work was a birthday cake: they were keeping Patti under wraps. But they couldn't really, with her shooting daytime television. And her Tony Alexander connection: that was bound to break any minute. Julie wondered about having a photographer on hand for the interview.

Tim's mind was running in the same channel. "Shouldn't we break this in the column, Julie? Or else give it to somebody downstairs. The boss-man won't like it if he finds out we're sitting on something as hot as this could be."

"The police are sitting on it too. I'm praying it holds that way till I get my interview."

"I hope it works," Tim said doubtfully. He turned back to the *Celebration* hand-out. "The only name I know—the director, Ed Cardova. I've met him a couple of times. He's one of those guys always about to do his big picture. Then somebody pulls out the money... Romulus Productions: wasn't Romulus a wolf?"

"Romulus and Remus, twin brothers who were nursed by a wolf. They founded Rome."

Tim handed back the literature. "Mafia money?"

"Shame on you," Julie said.

"Why not? There's art lovers among the Family—as you ought to know."

"Yeah." Julie was herself thinking of Morielli who didn't greatly take to the notion that the picture could escape the X-rating. As though that was where the money was. It wasn't. So why would he think so? Illogical, Julie. She had already thought of asking Sweets Romano about him, and then, uncomfortable with the idea, let it slip out of mind. One of these days she was going to have to face up to her feelings about Romano. "How do you face up to an ambivalence?" she asked.

"It's easy if you're two-faced."

"Thanks," Julie said and changed the subject. "Who are you taking to the theater with you?" She knew he had two seats.

"Would you have gone?"

"Yes."

"I wish I'd known. I'm taking her namesake. Who else, for God's sake. Our own Alice."

"You're a good boy," Julie said.

She walked back to the shop from Downey's, watching, for a little part of the way, Tim lope ahead of her. It was curtain time. She got an eerie feeling approaching the shop after dark, standing out in the open to insert keys into two separate locks. Nobody who knew its contents would try to burglarize the shop, but it had been broken into once and she had learned caution from that and other people's experiences. She did not enter until there were passersby, then she lit the lights and looked beyond the curtain into the back room before closing the outside door. But the precautions set her nerves on edge, and the rooms were cold and damp. She touched her hand to the radiator. Stone cold dead. By Halloween maybe, or Thanksgiving there'd be heat. After which the place would always be too damned hot.

From upstairs came a barrage of tiny footfalls and the screech of maternal wrath: bedtime for Juanita and her cousins. She found herself wondering what Mrs. Rodriguez would think of Patti Royce if she was at her window looking out when Julie brought the young actress here. There was nothing whorish about Patti, but what was that associable quality? No question it had to do with sex. She was also disarming. She kept thinking of the droop to Patti's wrist as she played her fingers inside the neckline of her dress. Was it instinctual or a calculated gesture? Come on, Julie: it was an instinct, the effects of which were calculable. Ron Morielli had been both provoked and appeased. Question. Who was Ron Morielli—besides being Patti's manager?

She jumped when the phone rang, a shattering noise in the quiet, sparsely furnished room.

"Julie, I'm in trouble. It's Eleanor. The police want to see me. They're sending a car."

She had quite forgotten that Eleanor had asked her to find a lawyer for her in case she needed one. "Now?" She asked.

"Yes. I don't know what mother's told them. She won't talk to me about it."

"Don't say anything until I've put you in touch with a lawyer. You have that right."

"Julie, I don't want a lawyer. I just want you to be there."

"I'm not equipped to advise you, Eleanor."

"I don't care."

"Is Fran home?"

"No."

"Don't leave the house till I get there. Understand? Make them wait."

TWENTY-SEVEN

THE UNMARKED CAR stood in front of the building. In the lobby Eleanor was waiting with her Saturday guards, Detectives Lawler and Ferretti.

"A family reunion," Julie said by way of greeting, and to Eleanor, "I thought we might get to talk for a few minutes here."

"It's all right," Eleanor said. "Inspector Fitzgerald agrees that you can advise me."

"I'll bet he agrees," Julie cried. "How does he know whether I can advise you or not? You won't even take the best advice I've got, which is to get a lawyer."

"Please, Madam," the doorman said. People were entering the building.

"Julie, I'm only going to tell the truth," the girl said with an air of reproach.

As it turned out, Julie and Eleanor had time alone together in the interrogation room of the local precinct house. It was a small, bare room with a table and four chairs, an air vent, no windows, chalk-white walls. A video tape machine stood in one corner. The ceiling lights were inset and could be raised, no doubt, to high intensity.

"What a place for a graffiti artist," Julie said, talking to break her own tension. Some advisor.

"Please don't worry about me," Eleanor said. "I'll tell the truth and try to make them understand."

"Stop saying that. Why didn't you tell it in the first place?"

"Because I didn't think anybody would believe me."

"And what's different now?"

"Something mother didn't tell anybody before. She thought I'd taken her revolver all right, but what she was afraid of was that I'd gone homicidal. I guess suicidal would have been all right. Anyway, she called the office and spoke to Tony and told him I might be on my way there. And I was. But I never got there. He was waiting for me, but I never got there."

"He was waiting for you?" Julie repeated.

"Mother says he was waiting for me. They talked on the phone."

"You did not kill him," Julie said.

"No. It was all make believe. I think. But she was right in the first place: I did take her gun."

"Eleanor, I can't advise you."

"Don't then. Just stay with me."

"TELL US in your own words, Miss Alexander," Marks said.

They sat at the table as though paired for bridge, Marks opposite Julie, the inspector leaning back, his arms folded, his eyes blue ice, opposite Eleanor. The video tape ran throughout.

"I hated him first because my mother loved him more than she did me. But most of all, for the way he treated me when I was a child. I thought this was a way I could get even. If you don't believe there was someone in the office with him when he called home, then it's hard to understand."

"I think we can agree there was someone there at the time, don't you, inspector?" Marks said.

Fitzgerald grunted assent.

"I imagined him there with this girl while he was asking me to tell Fran he needed another hour before he could get away..." She turned to Julie. "It doesn't sound convincing now, but I *was* sure."

"Tell us what you did," the inspector said. "Never mind the whys and wherefores of it for now, little lady."

"I left a note for my mother that I was going to a movie. On the way to the shop I fed a cat outside the apartment building and then two of them in front of the shop. It was in order to feed the cats that I went to the shop at all. Or that's what I thought of first, but on the way I thought about mother's revolver, and I had the keys to the shop and the alarm wasn't on." Eleanor stopped and frowned as though trying to clarify something. "I didn't even know if there were any bullets in it. You see, there's something I'm not really sure of: *when* was it that I thought of killing Tony..."

Oh, Christ, Julie thought: why mention it at all?

"...At first, all I wanted to do was break in on them, catch them right in the middle of—whatever they were doing. That would be true revenge."

Julie stopped her for the moment, putting her hand on the girl's arm. "Inspector, Eleanor has always believed that her step-father deliberately exposed her to a child molester when she was eleven years old."

There was no change of expression on the inspector's face as his eyes shifted to Julie and then back again to Eleanor. The information, as she had just put it, did Eleanor little, if any, good.

"I *know* it," Eleanor said. "It isn't that I have always believed. I have *known*."

"So you took the handgun," Marks prompted softly.

"It made me feel—strong. Just to have it in my purse, to feel the outline of it in my lap. I took a cab to Forty-second Street and Lexington. It was when I got out in the rain and somebody tried to pick me up outside the hotel near Tony's building that I became quite violent in my mind. I thought I'd been taken for a prostitute, you see, and that whole feeling came over me of guilt and revulsion and hatred, and I blamed Tony for it. I was sure I could kill him. And I wanted to. Oh, yes. He was with this woman, a young woman..."

"Who?" Marks interrupted.

"I don't know who," Eleanor said, furious at being interrupted. The vein was up in her forehead and both detectives noticed it.

"Go on," Fitzgerald said.

"I stood there wondering if I could get in the building, or if a guard would take me for a prostitute and stop me. I know about Security. And I know how big the building is, though I've never been in it at night. I walked all the way around it. I even tried the door, I guess it's on the south side, which is locked at night. I'm telling you all this although it doesn't mean anything. When I got back to where I'd started, I went into the hotel and phoned to make sure he was still there. The man in the next booth, I could see his watch where he was resting his arm on the partition: It was ten o'clock.''

She herself might easily have met Eleanor outside the building, Julie thought, but it would not have mattered, for not having yet met, they would not have recognized one another.

"When Tony answered the phone," Eleanor continued, "I didn't make a sound. I had my finger in one ear: I kept listening for the other voice, but all I could hear was breathing and then he hung up. I was so tense by then I spilled my change all over the shelf, and then I dropped my pocketbook and it had the gun in it. When someone tried to pick it up for me I grabbed it from him and ran.''

Marks and Fitzgerald exchanged glances. Julie guessed that the witness in the next phone stall had come forth, remembering the girl's behavior when he learned of the homicide. He would have put Eleanor near the scene so close to the time of Tony's death that the police had to consider her a prime suspect.

"I don't remember much about the next hour. I thought a lot about committing suicide. I must have run or walked all the way. I know I passed the movie house where *Stevie* is playing and felt saved. I must have unlocked the padlock on the grille and the shop door and I put the revolver in the drawer and then, like it happens in a dream, I was in the theater and I was terribly glad I got there before Stevie's aunt was old and going to die. When the movie was over and I got home and mother wasn't there everything about the whole night seemed even more like a dream, but the lids from two cans of *Nine Lives* were there and I couldn't find the note I'd written mother. When the police came and I discovered what had happened to Tony, I was afraid to tell the truth. I didn't even know the truth.''

"Have you told it now?" Marks asked.

"It is much ado about nothing, isn't it?"

"A man is dead and that isn't nothing," the inspector said. "You've a good deal to explain yet, little lady. No, indeed: We are not talking about nothing. You can't just say, 'like it happens in a dream.' That won't do, as experienced counsel will tell you. How do you know—admitting yourself to have been in a troubled state of mind—that you didn't actually gain access to the building, which is by no means security-tight—and let me say to you now from a long experience of the streets of New York, any man who took you for a prostitute would never have seen one—but how do you know you didn't take the elevator to... what floor was your step-father's office on?"

"You don't need to answer that," Julie said.

But Eleanor said, "Fifteen."

"To the fifteenth floor and finding him in his office, how do you know that in this same dream, you didn't kill him?"

"I don't."

"You don't know?"

"Not for absolute certainty."

SHORTLY THEREAFTER, Fitzgerald and Marks left the room. Going, Marks turned off the recorder and assured the young women that they were not being monitored.

"They don't understand, do they?" Eleanor asked as soon as the door closed.

"I'm not sure I do," Julie said. "What made you phone Tony from the hotel lobby?"

"Because I was afraid by then. I thought if I heard his voice, *their* voices, it might give me courage." Eleanor let her head loll back between her shoulders, her eyes closed. Then she came back to life. "That's not true. I turned to jelly with fear, and gave up. All I wanted when I made that phone call was to interrupt what I imagined they were doing. It was an obscene phone call inside out. I was being a dirty little child again..."

"Okay," Julie said. "I get it."

"Julie... are all prostitutes lesbians?"

"Ha! You know, people think I know all about prostitutes because I spend a lot of time in one of the neighborhoods and once I tried to help a street girl. But I don't know much. I've heard they often are."

"I'll bet some people think gay is worse."

"That's their problem," Julie said.

A few minutes later Marks returned alone. He sat where Fitzgerald had. "The inspector wonders if you'd consent to what's commonly called a lie detector test, Miss Alexander."

"Tonight?" Julie said.

"No, not tonight," he said impatiently. Then, to Eleanor: "We would also like to arrange psychiatric consultation."

"No," Eleanor said emphatically.

"If I may advise you, Miss, I wouldn't refuse out of hand. Buy a little time that way and get yourself a lawyer."

TWENTY-EIGHT

JULIE PROPOSED TO STAY only a few minutes when they got back to the Alexander apartment. Eleanor kept saying that if her mother was home she didn't want to face her alone.

Fran came out to the foyer in nightgown and negligée, her reading glasses in hand. She murmured an apology: she had felt on the verge of collapse after dinner. "I'm so grateful to you for going with her, Julie."

Julie glanced at the girl. Eleanor's eyes fell away like those of a child caught in mischief. She had deliberately lied about her mother's not being home. Julie made no response to Fran: it wasn't as though she'd gone to the dentist or the hair dresser with her daughter.

Fran offered coffee or cocoa. No one wanted anything. She suggested that they go into the living room.

"Not there," Eleanor pleaded.

"The picture can be restored. They took it away tonight," Fran said.

For once Eleanor said nothing.

They wound up in Fran's bedroom where, when she climbed back into the king-size bed, she looked small and frail. An open copy of Wilder's *The Bridge of San Luis Rey* lay on the pillow beside her bed rest. "I read it every few years," Fran said, "as though it foretold my own destiny." Both mother and daughter had a flare for the dramatic, not to say the melodramatic. Settled, she folded her hands in her lap. "Now tell me."

Julie sat at the foot of the bed on Tony's side, Eleanor on a chair near her mother. She couldn't seem to get started, so Julie said, "She's got to have a lawyer for one thing."

"Oh," Fran said as though she hadn't expected that.

"Julie's going to get her husband to recommend someone."

"I see," Fran said coldly, rejected. Then: "Do you have urgent need of one?"

"Mother, you were right. I did go to the shop after Tony called. And when you couldn't find the gun, it was because I'd taken it. And you were right when you called him and said I might come there. I intended to, but I didn't have the guts."

"You intended to go there," Julie said, "but not to kill him."

"Let her speak for herself," Fran said.

"I just wanted to break them up," Eleanor said.

"Break who up?"

"Mother, don't be stupid. The woman who was with him in the office. The girlfriend."

"How do you know she was there if you didn't go there?"

"I just know, that's all. I heard whispering on the phone. The police believe me."

"You don't know that they believe you, Eleanor," Julie said. "Why don't you try to tell the whole story to your mother now, just the way you told it to Lieutenant Marks and Inspector Fitzgerald."

It was the same story and yet it wasn't: in the first telling, the burden of hatred was on herself and Julie had believed her whether or not the detectives had, but in repeating it to her mother, the girl somehow shifted the emphasis to her loathing of Tony, and now it was obscene.

Julie watched a change come over Fran. Her eyes grew hard and remote, and there came a point at which she looked as though nothing she would hear could change her feelings against her daughter.

"It was like a dream," Eleanor told again. "I can hardly remember putting the gun away, but I'm sure I did. I must have."

Fran's grubby hands clutched the sheet. There was the look of an animal to her. And her voice had a low, rough sound, even a kind of menace. "He was about to come home when I spoke to him and then he waited for you."

"Fran, he was waiting before that," Julie said quietly.

"I felt so foolish," the woman went on as though she hadn't heard her, "when I found the gun, so ashamed of my fears of what you might have done. Even after what happened *had* happened, I would not tell the police."

"Why didn't you tell them, mother? What's made it so awful is both of us not telling. Why didn't you tell them?"

"Because the gun was there in the drawer and I thought I had misplaced it. I thought it was all in my own imagination. But I knew you better than I thought, didn't I, my daughter?"

"I didn't kill him, mother."

"He was waiting for you and he died."

"Fran," Julie tried again, "how long did he wait for Eleanor? It couldn't have been more than a half hour."

Fran shook her head that she did not know.

"He'd been waiting all evening for someone—from the time he first called home and said he'd be an hour late meeting you at the restaurant. He went back to the office to meet someone and it wasn't Eleanor. He took this man named Butts with him. I think because he was afraid, but I don't really know that."

"He said to me on the phone that he was about to come home," Fran repeated stonily. "Whoever he'd been waiting for had come and gone by then."

Julie threw up her hands. "He *said* he was about to come home. That doesn't make it the truth. The situation he was in isn't exactly truth inspiring, is it?" She made herself calm down. "All I'm saying, Fran, someone could have arrived after your call. Not only could have, *must* have. Didn't you phone back after you found the gun?"

"There was no answer then," Fran said.

"How long between your two calls?"

"The police have calculated it at a half hour. It was ten forty-five when I called back and didn't get him. I looked at my watch and wondered if he'd be home ahead of me. I wanted it that way, not my sitting here waiting for him. In fact, that's why I cleaned and polished the revolver, taking it apart and putting it together again—it was something that would occupy and delay me."

"Fran, did you know the person Tony was involved with?"

"Of course, I knew."

So, Julie thought, Doctor Callahan was right.

"You said you didn't want to know," Eleanor charged.

"What I have wanted lately has had very little relevance."

Julie put the question carefully: "What do you know of Tony's interest in a movie called *Celebration*?"

"Nothing," Fran said, "I didn't know he was interested—or for that matter that there *was* a film called *Celebration*." Her tired eyes wandered around the room as though looking for a place to settle. "I'm trying to remember—was it last spring? We were sitting on the terrace having a drink, and he asked me whether I thought an idea he had would make a good movie. Actually, it was about a farm family he knew as a boy. I didn't pay much attention. Whenever we needed money, he'd say he was going to write a screen treatment he was sure he could sell, but he never did it."

"What do you remember about the family in this story?" Julie prompted, her heart beating a little faster.

Fran's eyes came back to hers. "Was the girl retarded?"

"That's it," Julie said. She rummaged in her carry-all and brought out the proof of the advertisement. She gave it to Fran without comment. Fran put on her glasses.

Eleanor twisted around in her chair so that she could see it. "Yuk," she said.

Fran traced the copy with her finger as she read. The print was very small. "Oh, now—'Based on a story by David Clemens.' Julie, I'm quite sure that's the name Tony wrote under for a weekly newspaper before he came to New York. He made it up from the names of two writers..."

"Samuel Clemens and David Thoreau," Julie said.

"Of course!"

Julie felt on the verge of understanding something if only she could ask the right questions. At the moment the only thing she could remember about Tony's background was the dance marathon. "Fran, where did Tony come from?"

"A small town in Ohio you've probably never heard of, Albion."

She had heard of it, but for the life of her she could not remember where or when.

TWENTY-NINE

SHE WAITED until midnight to call Jeff. The concierge or whoever finally picked up the phone was not friendly. Five A.M., Paris time. Her husband wasn't any friendlier when she said, "Jeff? *C'est moi.*"

"What?"

"It's me, Julie."

"I know it's you, Julie. Do you know what time it is?"

"I was afraid I'd miss you later on. And you always say you can fall asleep anywhere, any time."

"What's happening?"

"I think she'll be all right, but I've promised Eleanor to ask you to recommend a lawyer." She recounted Eleanor's interrogation and the scene at home with Fran. Then: "Jeff, did you know Tony was serious about a young actress named Patti Royce?"

"I knew he was interested in someone young," Jeff said, and tried to get back on the subject of Fran and her daughter.

"I'm interviewing Patti Royce tomorrow afternoon."

"I met her once," Jeff said.

"Where?"

"I don't know where. With Tony."

"Thanks, chum," Julie said.

"I thought he'd get over it at the time. He half-thought so himself. In fact, I thought it was finished or I'd have mentioned it the last time we talked."

"Yeah."

"Julie, be fair: think of how things stood when I woke *you* up Saturday morning. The investigation had only started. Why hurt Fran unnecessarily—and be the source of that hurt—if the matter was irrelevant?"

"Why not trust my discretion?"

"I wish I had now. I'm sorry about that."

"So am I," Julie said. She was thinking back to their discussion at Sardi's on how well or ill either of them knew Tony; another time when it might have been told.

"There's a locker-room syndrome among adolescent boys which sometimes recurs with older men," Jeff said. "It has to do with so-called machismo."

"How boring."

"That's what it's about," Jeff fired back. "Boredom."

In similar snapping matches Julie customarily retreated, hurt. Now she said, "Jeff, do you ever go to Turkish baths?"

He burst out laughing, and then managed: "Every time I have wine on top of three martinis."

That brought them down more easily than seemed possible the moment before. But when he presently said that she was not to worry if he was out of reach for the next week, she instantly felt the pangs of concern.

"About the lawyer for Fran's daughter," Jeff said, "if it's up to you, why don't you call our attorney, Dave Lieberman? He'll give you a couple of recommendations."

"I should have thought of that myself," Julie said. The blockage was that she never thought of Lieberman as *our* lawyer. He had predated her in Jeff's life. "I'll call him in the morning. Jeff, did you know Tony wrote the story for a movie called *Celebration*?"

"I knew he always wanted to write one."

"It's a good picture and it stars Patti Royce."

"I hope Fran gets some money out of it, at least."

"I have another name to ask you about—Ron Morielli. Does it mean anything to you?"

"No."

"He's Patti's manager."

"The fast talking, high pressure kind?"

"Not much of a talker at all," Julie said. "I wish I knew more about him."

"Maybe you will after the interview."

"If I don't," Julie said, "there's something wrong with the whole set-up. And maybe that's what Tony was into."

"Something of that nature sounds more likely than his dying at the hands of either of those neurotic women in his own family."

"Or any of the other connections I was trying to make." She thought then of Butts and his saying he wouldn't want her marathon dance piece to fall into the hands of an evil-doer. "Jeff, Tony came from Albion, Ohio, a place I swear I've heard of recently, but I can't remember where."

"In one of the obituary columns?"

She almost had it then, but something else spun off from Jeff's suggestion: Tony saying to Tim Noble when Tim asked if they'd run anything about Jay Phillips, "You want to write obituaries? Write obituaries."

"Damn, damn, damn," Julie said. "I almost had it again. It's right in there with Jay Phillips and Morton Butts and City Councilman Whatshisname . . ."

"Julie, go to bed. Let it come to you. You can't go to it."

"David Clemens," Julie said.

"Who's he?"

"A pseudonym Tony wrote under before he came to New York."

"In Albion, Ohio?"

Fran hadn't actually said so, only that the paper was a weekly, and Julie had slipped in not asking for specifics—if Fran knew them. "I'll go after it tomorrow. Thanks, Jeff."

"What about the column? Is the *Daily* dropping it?"

"I forgot to tell you—Tim Noble and I are carrying on. It's now called *Our Beat*. I've got my own by-line, Jeff. Only I wish I'd got it under different circumstances."

" 'There is nothing dies but something lives,' " Jeff said, quoting a favorite poem. "I know we don't exchange cautions, Julie, but for someone to have taken Tony's gun away from him without a struggle took remarkable cunning."

Or persuasiveness, Julie thought. Which suggested murder by an intimate. And who was left after Fran and Eleanor? Patti Royce. Why hadn't Marks and Fitzgerald grilled *her*? Or had they?

THIRTY

JULIE WENT FIRST to Forty-fourth Street in the morning, wanting to drop off a tape recorder for the afternoon interview. She arrived to find Reggie Bauer, her Forum informant, sitting on an ashcan waiting.

"May I?" He hopped down and took the keys from her. He was a time diddling between the two locks.

Rose Rodriguez opened her window and leaned out to see what was going on. Julie greeted her cheerfully. Reggie, the door open, stepped back and saluted the woman upstairs. He asked Julie, "Does she have a solicitor's license?"

Julie lit up the two rooms. "Let me guess what you found out," she said. "The original Little Dorrit dropped out of the show for an abortion."

"That's not fair," Reggie said and pointed at the crystal ball. "You've been reading that bloody thing."

"Am I right?"

"That's the backstage scuttle. She was getting a lot too plump for a jailhouse stray, and that's not one of the symptoms of appendicitis. Now here's the added attraction: During rehearsal—that's five months ago—Abby developed such a passion for one of the chorus boys, the straight one, that she almost got him fired from the show. Whatever happened, he gave notice himself right after they opened. Which you must admit doesn't make much sense. He's the undeveloped character so far. I haven't had time to locate him. But now let me tell you about Abby's mother. They call her Madame Defarge, which shows how deep everybody is into Dickens, and Abby's out of the show temporarily, right? Well, Madame Defarge goes to the theater every night, takes her knitting, and sits outside the star's dressingroom."

"No kidding," Julie said.

"Not much. She's backstage every night and nobody's asked her not to come. She bad-mouths Trish Tompkins every opportunity she gets. And everybody says Tompkins is better than Abby Hill in the part. They say Michael Dorfman would like to see her take it over for good and maybe send Abby on the road with the National Company when it gets organized, but he doesn't dare."

"Actors Equity or Madame Defarge?"

Reggie smiled wistfully. "I'll try and find out, but inner Dorfman is a little out of my reach."

Which admission, Julie thought, gave Reggie Bauer credibility. Michael Dorfman wasn't going to take anyone with less than star status into his counsel. Unless he was compelled to.

"No. Let me take it from here, Reggie. You've done a great job. I talked with my partner. We can't really afford a legman, but if you want to go on a free-lance basis, we'll pay you twenty bucks for every item we use. How does that sit?"

"My mother's going to be so proud of me," Reggie said with such dryness you could almost hear the crackle.

JULIE CALLED David Lieberman who, first thing, congratulated her on *Our Beat* and remarked on now having two Hayes careers to follow. He gave her the names of two criminal lawyers and an order of recommendation after drawing her out on Eleanor.

"I think she's a bit strange," Julie said, "but not a murderer."

"Why don't you have her give me a ring and I'll set it up with whichever counsel she chooses. Is she a seemly chick?"

"Well, yes," Julie said, although it was not the description she'd have applied to Eleanor. Or anyone else, for that matter.

JULIE CALLED Eleanor and then weighed calling Marks on the various bits and pieces she had been able to pick up. She put it off until after the interview with Patti Royce. Her newspaperwoman's instincts were getting stronger.

On her way crosstown she stopped at 1440 Broadway where Michael Dorfman had his office. Dorfman, of whom it was said that in the old days when actors made the rounds, he'd come out from his inner sanctum and give those waiting in the lobby a two minute lecture on the state of the theater and on the importance to each of them of appearing in Equity Library productions. He was also known to have remarked to a critic that he had never hired an actor from an Equity Library production yet.

When Julie walked in he was handing the receptionist a stack of typing. He finished his instructions without a word, a smile, or a nod to Julie. She waited. In her acting days she would have shrunk so small you could have swallowed her with a glass of water.

"So you're the Tony Alexander replacement," he said without preliminaries. "You should call it the Phoenix Nest."

"Not bad," Julie said. It had been used often enough, but she didn't say that. "Could we talk for a few minutes, Mr. Dorfman?"

"Why not?" He looked at his watch.

She followed him into his private office where the phone was ringing. While he took the call Julie made a quick tour of the gallery of stars in bygone and current Michael Dorfman productions. If you didn't know who he was, she thought, you'd say you were in the office of a small town booking agent or a packager of summer road shows. Except for the pictures. The glamor was all up front. He was stingier with no one more than he was with himself.

"Looking for anyone special?" he asked, off the phone.

"Patti Royce."

"*Autumn Tears*," he said. "Look over next to Carol Channing." He joined her where she gazed at the over-wise child, her lips a provocative pout. "Is it true she's making a comeback in daytime television?"

"I've heard," Julie said.

"Well, it took Shirley Temple forty years and a California president.... Tell me, who do you think Patti looks like?"

She was not going to say Marilyn Monroe. "A kid wear-ing her first bra. I have an interview coming up with her. We'll be talking about *Autumn Tears*."

Dorfman cut off the incoming calls and sat down with Julie at a low table devoted to a stack of *Variety* dailies and an ashtray the size of a hubcap. He took a single cigarette from his inside pocket and lit it. He inhaled and let out a slow stream of smoke. "And Jay Phillips and his wife's su-icide and all that dead shit. What do you want from me, Julie?"

"The true story about Jay and why you fired him. I think it connects with Tony and I want to know where."

Dorfman sat, a stone monument with a live cigarette.

Julie said, "Let me put it together for you the way I see it: Jay did your publicity for a long time, one of the best in the business. Maybe you owed him a lot, maybe you're just a decent human being who felt sorry for a man with a problem. Jay had a real one: girls around the age of pu-berty, especially theater types. I don't know how far he got with Patti Royce, but I do know how far he got with Tony Alexander's step-daughter, and so did Tony. After every incident, and maybe there weren't all that many—I mean how many roles are there for girls of that age?—but every time something happened, Jay did penance, saw his priest, saw his doctor maybe, and swore it would never happen again, and drank more heavily than before. You might not even have known about it sometimes. The victims feel guilty too. But when the stage mother finds out, you've got real trouble. Take Madame Defarge: I'm going to guess now. Abby Hill got into trouble early; it wasn't with Jay Phil-lips, but Jay must have laid himself open. He must have been available when Abby's mother found out her star-child was pregnant, and Abby, not wanting to name the boy who had already left the show, or maybe to get even with Jay, blamed him. As I said, I'm guessing: Madame Defarge threatened to sue the management if her daughter's career was damaged, etcetera, etcetera. Abby came down with ap-pendicitis. But for you it was the last straw with Jay. Did he swear up and down that he was innocent?"

Dorfman opened wide his puffy, hitherto half-closed eyes and looked at her over another long pull and expulsion of smoke. "No comment," he said.

"Because I'm sure he was innocent. Of Abby's condition anyway. Child molesters are almost always impotent."

Dorfman looked as though he had found himself the butt of a bad joke. "Where does Tony Alexander come in?"

"I hoped you'd be able to tell me," Julie said.

Dorfman put out his cigarette. "You know, I've been around for a long time. I'm reminded of the old vaudeville joke about the Irishman just off the boat. A fella went up to him and said, 'Pat, can you tell us what time it is?' 'How did you know me name is Pat?' says the Irishman. 'I guessed it,' the fella said. 'Then,' said Pat, 'guess the time.'"

Julie left, chagrined and furious, but Albion, Ohio, had jolted into place: the "boys" of seventy or so at Jay Phillips' wake. One of them had been talking about his season many years ago at the Albion Playhouse.

And then, at the bottom of her carry-all, she found the *Times* obituary for Jay Phillips, which listed the Albion Summer Playhouse among his credits.

THIRTY-ONE

As MARY RYAN predicted they would, she and Julie found Jack Carroll at St. Malachy's Seniors' Center in the cafeteria lineup for lunch. The whole large room, which even Julie could remember as the Actors Chapel, was a lot more cheerful in its conversion; there were more lights, white garden furniture, and an aviary at one end. The public telephone was in what had once been a confessional box. Talk about sacrilege.

Mrs. Ryan selected a table where she seated Julie. "I'll go up and speak to Jack," she said. "And as long as I'm here I might as well have a bite and save having to fix for myself. Can I bring you something, dear? I don't think they'd quibble over a glass of tomato juice."

"No, thanks," Julie said. "I'm fine."

Mary Ryan got her ticket and insinuated herself next to Jack Carroll. She brought him to the table, both with their trays: pea soup, ham, potato and broccoli and a pudding that put Julie in mind of lunch at Miss Page's School.

Carroll shook Julie's hand and then, letting his soup cool, started to talk about himself to Mrs. Ryan. "Did I tell you, Mary, they called me from the New Irish Theatre for the revival of *Juno*? I told them right off I wasn't going to read for them. 'I've been in this business sixty years and if you haven't seen me in that time, it's your hard luck,' I said to him. Then this voice on the other end of the phone said, very polite, mind you, 'Mr. Carroll,' he says, 'I'm twenty-seven years old and this is my first job as a stage manager.'" Carroll paused to test the temperature of his soup.

"Was Jay Phillips stage manager at the Albion Playhouse?" Julie asked.

"He was," Carroll said, and continued his own story. "'In that case I'll come round and you can look me over,' I said and I did. He wanted me to read for the part of Needles Nugent. 'Not Joxer?' said I, for in my heart I've been Joxer all my life. And he said, still very polite, mind you, 'Mr. Carroll, don't you think Joxer is a little young for you?' 'Young man,' I said, 'Joxer is ageless and so is Jack Carroll.' Ach, it won't run anyway. There's nobody around today that can play O'Casey. Now that company Dorfman sent out—it was the summer of...well, it was about the time of the draft, I remember, 1940, was it?—we did *Juno*...and *The White Steed*. Ha! The farmers all thought they were coming to see a play about a horse... Mary, do you remember Bridie Meath? I was thinking about her the other day at the wake when I saw Mike Dorfman. She used to say about Mike, 'He's so stingy he could squeeze a ha'penny out of a mouse.' And look at him now: three shows on Broadway, and all of them hits.''

"He was loyal to Mr. Phillips, wasn't he?" Mrs. Ryan said, and gave Julie a nudge under the table.

"That he was. He's always liked the Irish. God knows why. He's never made a nickel out of an Irish play. We're not a money-making people, by and large, are we, Mary?''

"For the love of God, Jack, will you tell the girl what you remember about Jay Phillips and the Albion Theater?''

Carroll had a few schlurps of soup. Then he straightened his hunched, narrow shoulders. "It wasn't the sort of place you put in your memory book, Mary. It was as Godforsaken a town as I've ever been in this side of the Atlantic. There were two things going on in the town that whole summer, two things: the playhouse and a religious tent show, a revivalist preacher who led his followers down to the river's edge every Saturday morning and conducted wholesale baptisms.''

"What was his name, Mr. Carroll?''

"I couldn't tell you that, Miss. I wasn't among the converted. But I'll tell you who was—Jay Phillips. And I think I can tell you how it came about.'' He paused and picked up the soupbowl in both hands and gradually emptied it, removing his face from sight except for the ears, which stuck out like clay handles. When he put the bowl down he took a handkerchief from his breast pocket, dabbed his lips, and refolding the handkerchief, returned it to his pocket. "Jay had a drop taken one night, as the Irish say. It was a Sunday night and God knows where he found a drop in that town on a Sunday night, but he went along by himself—or with this girl he picked up, it was probably that—to the prayer meeting. Well, during the meeting, I heard tell, and I don't remember who told it, he persuaded the girl to walk out with him. And where did he take her? The only place they could find with privacy was the cemetery. And then, by God, if her parents and the preacher and a sheriff's deputy didn't find them there. We could all have been run out of town, you know, all of us bearing the onus of being strangers and actors besides. And the girl, it turned out, was a minor. But Jay converted, or as they say, he bore witness and was born again. The preacher—there, I almost had his name—stood by him and the charges were dropped and the whole thing kept out of the paper, the way it can only happen in a small town."

"Was his name Butts?" Mrs. Ryan asked, by then caught up on Julie's thinking. "Morton Butts?"

"No, it was nothing like that."

"He could have changed his name," Julie said.

"I never seen him myself to my knowledge," Carroll said. "Some of the company, including Bridie Meath, went down to see Jay baptized. But they're all gone now. Bridie died last year, may she rest in peace. All of us, being Catholics, thought it a great sin, him switching over that way, but we were grateful all the same.... Isn't Butts the name of the wee firebrand you were talking to after the funeral, Mary? Couldn't you ask him?"

"If he changed his name to Butts, I don't think he'd want to talk about it.... But, a friend of Mr. Phillips and a Born Again Christian, Julie, couldn't you chance their being the same until you find out different?"

Julie nodded. "Mr. Carroll do you remember the newspaper in the town?"

Carroll pulled at one of his marvelous ears. "Ah, it was a weekly, and a weakly weekly, if you know what I mean."

"Do you remember anything about it, any of the staff?"

"Dear girl, the staff couldn't have been much more than a man and a boy. I remember they gave us very nice notices. I kept mine in my portfolio for years. The trouble was very few people ever heard of Albion, Ohio."

"Tony Alexander grew up in Albion, Ohio," Julie said, "and what I'd like to find out is whether he worked on the newspaper there at that time."

"He grew up there, did he?" Carroll said with an air of wonder. "But then, why not? We all have to grow up somewhere. I think I'd remember all the same, seeing the *Tony Alexander Says* . . . column all these years in the *Daily*."

"How about the name David Clemens?"

"Ah, now that rings a bell. As soon as I can get to my trunk in the Willoughby storeroom, I'll have a look."

"Couldn't we go back there after lunch?" Mrs. Ryan said.

"Instead of playing bridge?" said Carroll.

"It is urgent, isn't it, Julie?"

"Very."

IT WAS AFTER THREE when Jack Carroll finally neared the bottom of the trunk and brought up his portfolio. The clippings of theater reviews were all neatly pasted in. But those appearing in *The Albion Messenger* bore the name of Andrew Mason as reviewer. Which did not prevent Mr. Carroll from reading them aloud. Julie and Mrs. Ryan were kneeling alongside him, the sharp edge of the open trunk making ridges in their elbows; an extension lamp hung over the lid, blinding them. Newspapers, to the depth of a couple of inches, covered the bottom of the trunk. Mrs. Ryan shielded her eyes with one hand and groped among the papers with the other.

"They're all duplicates of what I read you," Carroll said. "You'd never know when an extra would come in handy."

"Is there an *Albion Messenger*?" Julie asked.

"You've a longer arm than me, dear," Mrs. Ryan said. "You look. Give us the light, Jack."

"You don't mind, do you, Mr. Carroll?" Julie asked.

"Root away."

They could not take much rooting, the papers brittle, orange-colored and mottled with mould. Julie lifted them carefully. A Columbus paper, one from Louisville, another from Oil City, Pennsylvania, one from Wheeling, West Virginia, and before she reached the bottom, a copy of the four-page *Albion Weekly Messenger*.

Julie and Mrs. Ryan took it to a table alongside the washer-dryers and left Carroll to repack his trunk.

The front page carried stories of the war in Europe, of the local young men drafted, and of the General Motors plant about to be built on the old fairgrounds where at the present time the Reverend Jeremiah Fox was holding his summer encampment. Julie pointed out the name to Mrs. Ryan and she called across the basement to Carroll, "The Reverend Jeremiah Fox, Jack . . ."

"That's it! He's the one!"

Julie turned with great care to editorials on page two. The editor and publisher of the paper was Andrew Mason. An editorial recalled historic warnings against foreign entanglements . . .

"Oh, my God," Mrs. Ryan said. "Will you look at the price of a pound of coffee? And eighteen cents for a dozen eggs."

Among the social events on the opposite page was the entertainment column which included Mason's review of *The White Steed*, something Jack Carroll had already read to them. Julie turned to the back page. The top story was headed, *Fox Predicts Thousand Witnesses Saturday Dawn*. The reporter was David Clemens.

"Isn't that the name you asked him about?" Mrs. Ryan wanted to know.

"That's the name," Julie said. She had finally forged the link among Phillips, Tony Alexander, and the man she knew as Morton Butts.

THIRTY-TWO

"YES," FRAN SAID, "the Reverend Fox had a great deal to
do with the direction of Tony's life. And it's quite possible
Tony had something to do with his being run out of Albion. That's something even a loving Christian would find
hard to forgive. Are you sure it's the same man, Julie?"

"Almost certain."

"But Tony hadn't mentioned him for years. I don't think
he even knew he was in New York."

"Probably not until they came face to face at the may-
or's birthday party."

"Of course. I'm very slow. You must forgive me."

Julie shook her head that there was nothing to forgive,
and waited. They were sitting in the living room, their backs
to the bare wall where Tony's portrait had hung. The
opaque curtains were closed, but Eleanor was a shimmer-
ing silhouette where she sat reading on the terrace in the afternoon sun. Calmly waiting for the next police move.

"I wish my mind would clear," Fran went on. "There
must have been hatred between those two. I remember
Tony's saying there wasn't much difference between fox and
skunk when it came to smell. You have to take into account
what the country was like at the time—just before World
War Two, isolationism, patriotic and religious fervor—not
that I was paying that much attention myself, not at the age
of three. But I think we can get the best idea of it if we think
of the 'moral majority' closer to our own times."

"Got it," Julie said.

"Tony had already tried to strike out on his own—to get
away from Albion. I may be wrong on dates, but I know it
had to be earlier because on that occasion he got as far as
Pittsburgh and went broke. This is a story I heard many
times: he partnered with a hymn-singing girl from Chey-

enne, Wyoming, in a dance marathon. Tony always said she prayed them through the horrors. The rowdies in the audience taunted them—'Ride 'em, cowboy!' That sort of thing. They won two hundred dollars, but Tony's health broke down and he went back home. I think that's when he got the job on the newspaper. He swept floors, made coffee, even set type—Tony the 'gopher.' I suppose that's why he wanted a fancier name for his by-line.

"About Jeremiah Fox—the way I remember hearing it—with his fundamentalist preaching and showcase baptisms (Tony's words, but not at the time, of course), he emptied the churches that summer, all except the Roman Catholics. And there weren't many of them in Albion. I won't go into why Tony distrusted Fox—I'm not sure I know its origins—but he wrote a story, and set it in type himself, which he called an exposé of religious fakes. I think he probably said there was more true religion in the girl from Cheyenne. But Fox was very popular and he struck back. It got the publisher into real trouble. Tony lost his job. He went back to work on the farm. His brother had been drafted by then, the one who later died at Guadalcanal.

"Then something happened with the Reverend Fox that turned things around. He was given a baby to baptize and he accidentally drowned it. The town turned on him like that." Fran snapped her fingers. "Tony said he'd never forget the child's father carrying his body up from the river and saying over and over, 'He killed my sweet little baby boy.'"

"Oh, boy," Julie said.

"The Reverend Fox left town without even waiting to take down his tent. After a while Tony was offered his job back on the paper, but by then he was ready to leave for good. He packed his typewriter, books and clothes into his 1931 Chevvy and drove to New York. He sold the car for eighty dollars when he got here and lived on the money for three months. I don't think he left Manhattan again."

"Did he ever talk about meeting Jay Phillips, the press agent, back in Albion?"

"No, Julie. He did not," Fran said emphatically.

Julie dropped the subject. "Any word from the police?"

"Only to check this morning to be sure that she's still at hand." Fran indicated the figure on the terrace. "Are you going to tell them about Jeremiah Fox?"

"Unless you want to."

"I have nothing to gain but more heartache by seeking them out," Fran said. "Do what you think you must."

THIRTY-THREE

JULIE TOOK A CAB crosstown to the Ninth Avenue Studios where she was supposed to pick up Patti Royce at six. People were leaving the building in bursts, frantic for taxis. Julie kept the one she had. Six o'clock passed; five minutes, ten minutes, and no sign of Patti. The cabbie grumbled even though the meter was on his side.

Patti Royce drifted out of the far door looking back as she left the building and again before getting in the cab.

"Let's go," Julie said to the driver.

His acceleration rocked them back in their seats. Then he adjusted the mirror to get a better look at his new passenger.

"I don't know why they don't make me wear mufti or a sari or whatever it is the Arab women have to wear when they go out in public." She mimed a swirl of something around her head.

"They?" Julie said.

"I'm supposed to crash onto the scene next week an instant winner." She temporarily ignored Julie's question. "Money, money, money." She laid her fingers with blood-red nails on Julie's wrist. "Don't get me wrong, I love money. *They* are my manager, the producers and my agent. Does that make a conglomerate? It used to be fun, like a game: You make this move and Patti goes ahead six places. Only it's not fun now without Tony." She turned and looked out the rear window. "I'm not supposed to give interviews unless they okay it."

"It's not as though I work for *Hustler* or *The Daily Worker*," Julie said.

"It's not you. And ordinarily I don't mind playing hard to get to, but I've been dying to sit down and talk to someone who knew Tony. I just wish they'd get me out of this fucking soap opera." Her adjective had the impact of the word coming from the mouth of a child, something she knew the effect of but not the meaning. An illusion which she had intended, Julie realized. Patti was a long way past innocence.

"Were you in love with Tony?"

"We were going to be married. I called him daddy. That kind of tickled him. In love, honey? What does it mean?"

Julie took a chance. "Any thoughts on who killed him?"

"Well, yes now. I do have." She turned and looked gravely at Julie. "We haven't begun the interview yet, have we?"

"If that's the way you want it, no."

The cab turned into Forty-fourth Street and Patti was distracted, looking out the window. "That's the Actors Forum, isn't it?"

"That's it. Ever been there?" They'd have had to break off in any case, about to arrive at the shop.

"Once. An actress I was in a play with took me there."

"Madge Higgins?" Julie said, naming the actress who had first called her attention to Patti: she had played her mother in *Autumn Tears*.

"Do you know her?"

Julie nodded. "I saw her the other day. She's working in something at the Forum."

"Will you give her my love? I was such a brat and she was just as nice as she could be. My mother hated her."

"Let's talk about *Autumn Tears* when we get inside," Julie said as the cab drew up to the curb. "This is it, my office away from the office."

Julie was quick but Patti was quicker. She whipped twenty dollars out of her pocket and stuck it in the cabbie's cash box. She didn't wait for change. Julie would have liked to, but she didn't. "I just got my allowance," Patti explained.

Mrs. Rodriguez practically dropped both breasts over the windowsill, leaning out to get a better view while Julie opened the shop door.

As soon as Patti saw the crystal ball, she said: "Is that what I think it is?"

"The last tenant was a fortune teller, among other things."

"Can you read it? Tell my fortune, Julie. There's things I've just got to know." She sounded in earnest.

"I'm strictly a phony," Julie said.

"I don't care. I need to be told something I want to hear."

Julie motioned her toward one of the chairs. "How about a cup of tea?"

"I'd adore a cup of tea."

"You don't mind if I call you Patti?"

"I wouldn't answer if you didn't. I don't like the name Royce, but Mum changed it from Roczinski before there was a Polish pope. I wanted to shorten it to just Rosen, but Mum said there were too many Rosens already. Besides . . ." She decided against finishing the sentence.

Julie filled the kettle at the bathroom sink and returned with it. "What about your mother? A strong lady, right?"

"Until she died and went to heaven. Or someplace."

"Let's turn on the tape recorder," Julie said. "Then after I write it up, I'll show it to you before publication. Okay?" She added the qualification at a startled look from Patti.

"We'll have to get Ron and Ted's okay."

Julie set the machine rolling. "Ron and Ted: they sound like a team."

"Ron's my manager. Ted's my agent."

"Do you need both of them?"

Patti shrugged. "They need each other." She kicked off her pumps and put her feet up on the coffee table. Her red toenails shone through her hose.

"How did they get along with Tony?"

A mistake: Patti looked up at her and then away with a downward sweep of her head.

"Strike that," Julie said, "and let's take the next question."

"Can't we just talk, and maybe you take notes the old-fashioned way?" Even as she spoke, Patti got up and went in her stocking feet, to the tape recorder. Near-sighted, she bent close until she found the right button and switched it off. No problem making that decision, Julie thought. Patti said, "Ooooo," as she went back to the chair and put her feet up. "Don't your feet get cold on this floor?"

"Yes," Julie said.

For some reason that struck both of them as funny.

"What was it you asked me?" Patti said. "How they felt about Tony? They were jealous of him, and I don't think it bothers them much that he's gone. As long as nobody asks them questions about it."

"Has anyone asked them questions?" Julie said carefully.

"What I mean is they're the kind of people who don't want to get involved. I don't always say things the way I mean. Ron thinks I'm dumb, but I'm not. It's sometimes better to play dumb. The police asked *me* questions...about where I was and all that. I was home, waiting for Tony to call me and say everything was set."

"Everything," Julie repeated.

"I'm speaking about the divorce," Patti said with a chilly directness.

"Remember what you said in the cab about having an idea who might have killed him?"

"It could've been his step-daughter and if Tony was alive he'd say so too. She was in love with him, and when she was younger she was so jealous of her mother they had to send her away."

Oh, boy.

"Did Tony believe that?" Julie asked and tried to turn herself around in order to evaluate the situation from that perspective. Was it Doctor Callahan who had also suggested that possibility?

"I don't know why he'd say it to me if he didn't."

"So that it wouldn't bother you that he was forty years older than you?" Julie suggested.

"I adored him being forty-two years older."

"How did you feel about Fran?"

"I didn't feel anything about her. If you got a man and you want him, you try and hold him, and if you can't hold

him, you might as well let him go, 'cause he's going anyway.''

"That's one way of looking at it," Julie said.

"You think I'm not very moral, don't you?"

Julie shrugged. "I'm a great suspender of judgments."

Patti thought about that. "Meaning you can't afford to
have an opinion that gets in the way of work?"

"All right," Julie said and got up. The kettle was coming to a boil. And it was time they got to the more conven-
tional interview materials—childhood, school, home, pets,
hobbies and when first did you want to be an actress? Oh,
God.

"Even a secret one?" Patti was still on the subject of
opinions.

Julie brought the tea. "I do have opinions I keep to myself."

"I have lots of them," Patti said, "but that's because I
need to keep changing them."

"You really did want to marry Tony, didn't you?"

"Yes." The lower lip shot out. "But don't ask me why
because if I tell you it probably won't be the real reason. I
met Tony first when he came to the Irving Theater to interview me during *Autumn Tears*, but you know I don't remember that time at all?"

"Do you know why you don't? I mean when somebody
as young as you draws a blank it often means they wanted
to forget. Say, you hated the play or the part or somebody
in the company..."

Patti gazed at her over the top of the steaming mug.
"Sweetie, you have to be just about the smartest woman I
ever met."

Julie shook her head. "In a court of law it would be called
the witness. I did a lot of homework. Let's get off the main
track for a few minutes and talk about Jay Phillips. All
right?"

"I don't want to much, but if you say so.... He's dead
and Mum's dead and that poor awful wife of his...and now
Tony. And in a way, I almost died. My career, I mean, and
I don't mean that's more important than human life. But

you could look at it one way and see how unlucky I am to people. I don't suppose Mr. Phillips would ever have wanted sex from me if I wasn't the way I am, and that was what he wanted."

"He might have," Julie said.

"That's what Tony said: it was like a disease and he'd had it for a long time, as long as Tony ever knew him. I used to think my mother gave me to him—like in exchange for all the publicity he could do for me, and she wanted him to show a play to his money contacts before I got too old for the part."

Julie harked back to Eleanor's conviction that Tony had given her to Jay. Did it go with the violation? A way to alleviate the guilt? "Did you feel guilty?"

Patti thought about it. "About doing what I did with him? No. I'd have felt more guilty if I hadn't done it. But that's me. Julie, what was your mother like?"

"Well . . . she's been gone for years and I'm only beginning to understand her. I used to think she steered me into marriage with Jeff because she wanted him herself."

"Isn't that interesting?" Patti murmured, fascinated. "Did she teach you how to flirt with him?"

"No . . . she went to the other extreme—trying to make sure I hung onto my virginity till my wedding night."

"Oh, wow."

"It was already too late," Julie said. "But not by much."

"Tony would say virginity is out of style."

"After one wearing," Julie said. "What about Jay's poor awful wife?"

"She was about as creepy a person as I ever met, and you got to believe I meet a lot of spooky types. Mum and I had an apartment in the East Fifties during the run of the play, and you know what she did? She came to see Mum and me to beg our forgiveness for what Jay did to me. Honest to God, Julie, the man went home and confessed to his wife and here she comes."

"Had you told your mother before?"

"Never, but like I said, I felt she'd planned it. And when his wife was saying how he felt so terrible and was going to take treatment and about how she'd forgiven him.... Oh, gosh, it was awful. And what did my mother do? She turned around and told the silly woman she was going to make such a stink. In other words she was going to take advantage of what happened to get what she wanted. You got to know—my mother was the pits."

"I got it," Julie said.

"And you know what happened then, don't you?"

"Mrs. Phillips went to the top of your building and threw herself off the roof."

"When I heard about that it was like I jumped some place too. I wasn't a child actor anymore after that. I did the movie, but they changed it a lot. They were looking for another Marilyn Monroe. I'm not that and I know it."

"You're a very special actor in *Celebration*," Julie said.

"Like I was making up for lost time." Patti smiled—a most winning smile. "Julie, I'm going to give you an exclusive: Do you know who wrote the story for *Celebration*? The screen credit says David Clemens, but that's a made-up name. Tony wrote it."

Julie felt so glad Patti Royce had told her that she could have cried. She needed very much to believe in her, but the supposed revelation came so suddenly that all she could say was, "Oh, well, now."

THIRTY-FOUR

"HE KNEW A GIRL just like her on the farm when he was a kid. Her father would go wild when the kids would tease her, and he'd beat the son for not standing up to them. Tony changed it a little."

"I've got to tell you I did know about the pseudonym," Julie said. "I showed Fran the ad that's going to appear in next Sunday's paper and she spotted the name right away."

"I'm glad you told me. I scared myself giving that out to you. But I just wanted somebody to know. They were thinking of treating this David Clemens as just another guy who wrote a story Mr. Bigshot Cardova turned into something real. I guess we ought to have this off the record, huh?"

Julie laughed. "Could be."

"Anyway, now that she knows Tony's made-up credit, they won't be able to keep it a secret."

"I don't understand why they'd want to," Julie said.

"I keep telling you, they're the kind of people who don't want to get involved. Tony didn't die a natural death, did he?"

"Patti, who else does Ron Morielli manage?"

Patti took several sips of tea. "I don't want to talk about Ron. Tony said he was counting on me to make him rich and famous and that's all right with me...now that Tony's gone."

"How did you find out about his death?"

"The police called me the next morning. I didn't believe it right away. It was a nightmare I couldn't wake up from. I'd stayed up all night learning next week's lines...and wondering why Tony didn't call me. Then I took a Seconal at five A.M.

"And it still doesn't seem real. Look at me. I got no more tears in me than a mannequin. Maybe it means I didn't love him after all. I just wanted him to take care of me. Or maybe I can't cry over real things, only when I make believe."

"How did you land in the soap—what's it called?"

"*Forgotten Splendor*. Doesn't that just make your heart go thumpity-thump?"

Julie grinned.

"Well, first came Tony telling me the story we called *Celebration*. First it was going to be *Birthday Celebration*. Anyway, I got him to tell it to Ron then, and Ron liked it. He didn't like it really. He says it's sick, but he knows what I can do and so he liked it for me and he knew a producer and people with money and so forth. We shot most of the film on a potato farm on Long Island with some ducklings the prop department borrowed and never did return. They couldn't catch them. I drove to upstate New York with the camera crew and the director and got introduced to my first cow. I must say, there ought to be an easier way to get milk.

"It all took about two months and everybody was great friends until they began to edit the picture and somebody thought they had something special. After that it was one thing after another, everybody quarreling with one another. Tony said I should keep out of it.

"He said I had to have an agent again and Ron finally agreed. I was flying. I was living a new life and I'd done it myself without dear Mum, and then Ted Macken came into the picture—Creative Talent, Inc.—and it was his idea that the daytime public, that means women, ought to get some kind of image of me before *Celebration* was released, and he knew of this part coming up in a daytime serial."

"I got it," Julie said. She had scribbled questions on a note pad, but she didn't want to turn Patti off.

"He said he could get them to write me out of it after a while." Patti drained the mug of the last of her tea. Just as she set it down, somebody pounded on the door. Impatient, whoever it was moved to the window and rapped with something as hard as stone. Patti moistened her lips. "Don't answer," she said. "Let's pretend there's nobody here."

"Won't work," Julie said, and pointed toward the ceiling as she got up. "I've got a neighbor you can buy with a button."

"I'm not supposed to give interviews."

"Let's deal with it." Julie went to the window in front. Ron Morielli was making the clatter with a money clip from which he had not removed the money. His sister waited at the door. Julie opened it on the latch, then slipped that.

"We come to pick up Patti," Morielli said, pushing in ahead of his sister, in case Julie tried to close the door on him, she supposed. "The kid's got an engagement she must've forgot about." He headed straight for the back room.

"Hello, again," Mrs. Conti said and followed her brother. She was wearing a lot of mink.

Julie missed whatever exchange occurred between Patti and Morielli because Mrs. Conti, in very high heels, slipped on the painted floor and caught hold of the curtain that partitioned the rooms. It ripped out of several rings. Julie helped the woman stay on her feet.

"Damn! I've twisted my ankle. Ron?"

"Get her jacket," he said, without looking round. And to Patti: "Come on, kid. Pick it up and let's go."

Mrs. Conti limped across the room and got Patti's jacket from the halltree where Julie had hung it.

"She's going to write up everything and show it to us before it goes in the paper," Patti said, conveying neither fear nor command in her voice.

"Yeah," he said, and to Julie: "We're trying to keep her under wraps for a while. I'll level with you, Mrs. Hayes: till the Tony Alexander story cools. I mean we want all the publicity we can get, but not that kind. We got nothing against you, you understand."

She'd been under wraps before Tony's death, according to Patti, but his version sounded credible.

"Patti," Julie said, "why don't you phone me when you're ready to finish the interview?"

The sister, meanwhile, had spotted the tape-recorder and called Morielli's attention to it.

"Why don't we all sit down and have a listen?" Morielli said.

"We didn't use the tape," Julie protested, well aware that Patti had cut it off at the question of how Ron and Ted felt about Tony.

Morielli said, "Let's take it along, Sis."

"It's my property," Julie said.

Morielli smiled and tossed his head toward Patti. "The kid's mine. How about that?"

"Ron, you shouldn't say things like that," Mrs. Conti removed the tape and rewound the few turns by hand. "He's only kidding, Mrs. Hayes. I promise to replace this." She tucked the tape into her pocket.

Patti put on her shoes. "Julie, that was the best cup of tea I ever had." Whatever her qualities, poise was high among them. "Ron, she knows about David Clemens."

"What else?"

"Ask her."

Morielli shifted his gaze to Julie. "You going to blow all this in the *Daily*?"

"Somebody's going to blow it soon, whether it's me or not. I'd be glad to have your version, Mr. Morielli. We could even tape it."

Morielli gave Patti's shoulder a rub as though for good luck. "We got a motion picture that's going to make fifty million dollars, and we're going to cut Tony's widow in for his share. Right, Patti? And maybe we should give her a cut of your share. How about that?"

"I couldn't care less," Patti said. She tossed her jacket around her shoulders and walked with a kind of swagger to the front door.

The other two followed her, having to step around the dangling curtain. It was pretty crowded where they waited for Julie to let them out. The silence was so eerie while she drew the latch, she glanced around. Morielli had his hand under Patti's jacket, apparently twisting her arm. Patti forced a grimace of pain into a smile for Julie's benefit. Morielli covered, too, by putting his cheek to Patti's. "The kid's all right, isn't she?" He winked at Julie.

"You bet."

JULIE FOUND HERSELF shivering after they had gone. The brother-sister act was scary. So was Morielli's masked menace, and Patti's mix of flare and submission. She did a haphazard job of stitching the curtains. She pricked herself twice with the needle. Very edgy. Call it scared, Julie. She kept hearing Morielli repeat, "What else?" to Patti. What else had she told Julie. Therefore, what else was there to tell that he hadn't wanted told? She telephoned Homicide, not knowing what she would say to Marks, but wanting reassurance from someone whose place was fixed. That was her greatest trouble: things, people, kept breaking loose when she thought she had them pegged. Marks was off duty.

Someone upstairs turned on the radio full blast. The whole building throbbed with Latin rock. You couldn't even hear the children crying. Or a scream if you needed to give one. She called the office on the chance that Tim might be there. It was seven thirty. No answer. Something told her to get out of the shop and she could not convince herself that it was imagination. She gathered notes and note book into her carry-all and took off. On the street she shed much of her anxiety, and by the time she reached the Village her fears seemed to have been ridiculous.

All day she had carried Gus' skewers wrapped in a napkin at the bottom of her carry-all. She delivered them and had a coffee at the counter. Gus tried to persuade her to have dinner. He'd made the day's specialty himself, moussaka. Julie said she couldn't eat anything. He gave her a lecture on anorexia, a disease from which he'd never known a Greek woman to suffer...so why give it a Greek name? Call it something American.

Julie wished she had tried the moussaka.

THIRTY-FIVE

WHEN SHE SAW the man waiting on the steps at Sixteenth Street, her heart began to thump. She crossed the street and approached her house, obscured from view by the parked cars. When he shielded his eyes from the street lamp the better to see her, she was tempted to turn back. Then she recognized Tim Noble. They started toward each other and had to stop for a spurt of traffic. Again the intrusion of the ridiculous, so that she was almost helplessly glad to see him.

"Are you running scared, Julie?" he asked.

"A little," she admitted, getting out her keys.

"I've been waiting almost an hour," Tim said.

"The phone won't do?" She collected the mail.

"No." He held the mail while she opened the inner door and followed her upstairs. In the apartment, as soon as Julie had turned on some lights, he said, "I saw *Celebration* tonight."

"And?"

"Patti Royce used to work at the Tripod. You know, the Turkish bath?"

Julie was surprised and yet not surprised. "So that's where Tony met her."

"I never met her myself, but I saw her there: very special. Julie, we've got to break something about her or be scooped by every jabberwock in town."

"I know.... I like that, jabberwock."

"I made it up after *Alice*. It's what we do, right?"

"Did you like *Celebration*?"

"The story's kind of old-fashioned, but that isn't going to matter much with all that bottled up sex in it."

Julie decided to hold back on the identity of David Clemens. To tell him would only increase the pressure he could put on her.

"And I liked her," Tim added, "but I had trouble drawing the line, if you know what I mean."

"I don't."

"Between art and . . . whatever."

"I see."

"I mean it's a porn film. Let's face it. Soft, maybe, but porn."

"I'm not so sure." Julie the expert.

"Julie, all I want to know: why can't I run something like this: 'The once and future star, Patti Royce, did some real life research for her soon-to-be released . . .'"

"No," Julie interrupted. "Absolutely not."

"Because of Tony?"

"Mostly."

"We don't have to do a one-two on it, for God's sake. How long are you going to sit on this thing? It's ready to hatch now if you'll get off the nest. Did you get the interview?"

"I got a lot."

"So?"

"Tim, does a man named Ron Morielli have anything to do with the Tripod?"

"Sure. He owns it." Then, slowly: "Oh? Romulus Films?"

"I think so," Julie said. "He and his sister broke up my interview with Patti."

"Is she an amazon-type blonde with Groucho Marx eyebrows?"

Julie nodded.

"I've seen her around."

"Are they Mafia, Tim?"

He shrugged. "Ask your friend Romano."

"Thanks."

"I still say we got to break the story, Julie."

"Did you find anything out about the production? Did you talk to the director? You said you knew him."

"I just saw the picture a couple of hours ago."

"Let's hold out until tomorrow noon. Okay?"

"You want to talk it over with the cops, right?"

"Approximately right."

Tim threw up his hands. "What do you care about *Our Beat*?"

Julie didn't answer.

"What do you care about it, Julie?"

"Tim, let's not quarrel. Are you hungry?"

"I'm always hungry."

"I'll make sandwiches. How about a beer?"

"Couldn't you get hold of Lieutenant Marks while I'm still here?"

"Let me fix the sandwiches and I'll try, but I know he's off duty."

Julie rummaged through the cans in the kitchen cabinet and came out with Alaskan crabmeat. Tim was allergic. They divided a can of sardines.

"Hey," Tim said, looking around. It was his first time in the Hayes apartment. "I should have worn a tie."

"Jeff does most of the time."

"Even in bed?"

"You are not always humorous, Tim." She was stalling, half dreading to call her service or to try to reach Marks. When the phone rang she was glad that Tim was with her.

"Miss Julie?" Only one person . . . "This is Romano."

"Yes, Mr. Romano." She looked at Tim, a skittering glance that caught him puffing out his cheeks at the name; she looked at her watch. It was ten past ten.

"Am I intruding? Forgive my calling you at home, but my man tried your office numbers without success. I presumed to worry."

"I'm fine," Julie said, as tense as a drawn bow. Why was he worried? *If* he was worried. They were not in touch that frequently.

"I don't often see your newspaper, I admit, but I am informed that you are carrying on Mr. Alexander's column. I should have thought you could do better. There, I am being presumptuous."

"I appreciate your concern," Julie said. Oh, Christ. Never before had he made small talk with her on the phone. Always to the point instantly and off.

"And there must be a certain hazard to that occupation. I very much doubt the police are telling all they know about Alexander's death. In fact, normally intelligent reporters sound as though they have been computerized on gobbledygook...

"And your investigation of the Garden of Roses, how has that got on?"

"I've pretty much dropped it, Mr. Romano. Tony didn't like what I turned in."

"Really? The gentleman in occupancy would seem a likely subject. I admire his courage—or perhaps it's faith—in undertaking his small war on narcotics." Another Romano pipeline had been tapped. "Quixotes always interest me. I was hoping you might bring him to see me if the occasion presented itself."

"It might happen," Julie said, "when things get straightened out." She didn't believe it would, and neither did he, she felt. But she knew now he was not making small talk. She simply had not yet got the message.

"There is no hurry."

Julie plunged. It was the only way to turn things around, to handle her own anxiety. "Mr. Romano, have you seen a motion picture called *Celebration*?"

Tim waved his fist over his head in approval.

Romano chuckled. "I have seen it. It was screened here for me, perhaps a week ago. If I had known you were interested I could have arranged your seeing it here."

"I've seen it," Julie said. If it had been screened for him he knew everything there was to know about it—a good deal more than she did. "I think it's great."

"I'm so glad to hear you say so. The question is how to exploit it, wouldn't you say?"

"Is it pornography or is it art? That's one question."

"Art is never pornographic, Miss Julie."

"Then why was I asked in the screening room whether I thought it should be X-rated?"

"Because that's the way your inquisitor thinks," he said and then resumed his tone of gentle persuasion. "If you find it great, as you say, we are speaking of art. I hope it will be accessible to the general public. Many will not understand it, but it will explain themselves to a good many people who are in despair over their own eccentricity.

Julie made a noise of tentative agreement. Was this the very way he had intended their conversation to go when he called? Was this text, or sub-text?

"Do you know the young man who wrote and directed it?"

Wrote and directed: from a story by David Clemens.

"No."

"Then I must arrange a meeting: Eduardo Cardova. He deserves your attention. Very sensitive."

"Eduardo Cardova," Julie repeated for Tim's benefit. Then another plunge: "I'm doing an interview with Patti Royce for the Sunday magazine if her manager lets it happen."

"Is she articulate?"

"Oh, yes."

"She must find it satisfying to talk to a woman of sympathy."

"Someone who knew Tony."

"I forbore asking whether you would mention that misalliance in your interview, given the unfortunate circumstances."

There seemed to be nothing he did not know. Julie waited.

"It may interest you to know I was what they call the 'swing' investor in the project, Miss Julie: money that attracts money."

"I see," Julie said, shocked although she knew at once she ought not to be. But suddenly she had become aware of a situation that might account for Tony's violent reaction to her Garden of Roses story. "To answer your question, Mr. Romano, if I don't mention the relationship between Patti Royce and Tony Alexander, someone else will. It's bound to come out."

"In time, perhaps. But time, although you are too young to know it, is both arbiter and healer. You will do what you must do, I know, but let me suggest something to you. I know it's presumptuous, given what you know of my filmic and photographic interests, but I beg you to consider: any sensational association among the principals will condemn the picture to the very fate you and I would save it from. I may be contradicting myself to say that beauty is in the eye of the beholder—it also being true of what is not beautiful—but if this picture is released in a flurry of scandal, it will have no audience except a numerous body of scandal mongers. You might also want to consider Alexander's wife who has been both betrayed and bereaved, and further, if I am right in my interpretation of the gobbledygook, her daughter is under suspicion of the murder—surely more than a woman ought to bear."

"I am aware, Mr. Romano."

"I'm sure you are. Forgive me."

"I am also aware," Julie said, "that the story credit, David Clemens, is a pseudonym for Tony Alexander."

There was a second of silence, then: "Thank you for telling me."

"Didn't you know it?"

"Oh, yes, I knew. I'm merely thanking you for being so frank with me. Until I have arranged with Cardova then." He hung up.

"Tell me where the booze is and I'll get you a drink," Tim said.

Julie shook her head.

"Then I'll get me one. You didn't tell me the pseudonym bit."

"Didn't I?" she said, and let it go at that.

She went into Jeff's study and taped her best recollection of Romano's conversation, asking Tim to listen.

"You mean he really talks like that?" Tim said afterwards.

"I couldn't make it up if I tried. What do you think he was saying?"

"I always thought when people like him had something to say, boom, boom, and they'd said it."

"There was a warning in there of some kind, no question. And he was very touchy about Patti, the scandal part.

Do you suppose it could have to do with her stint at the Tripod?''

"How would he know about that?"

"Believe me, if she did it, he'd know about it."

"It was you who brought up the subject of *Celebration* with him," Tim reminded her.

"But he chuckled when I did."

"So he chuckled. What does that mean?"

"That I got where he was going ahead of him. It was *Celebration* that he called about: I'm more and more sure of it."

"Art is never pornography. He ought to know, right? The king of porn."

"Oh, Tim," Julie said, "I think I know. I'll bet anything Patti Royce made a porn film at some time, the hard core variety."

"And somebody's going to exploit it if *Celebration* is a hit, so Romano's trying to buy time to head them off. Or is he doing the exploiting?"

Julie laid her hand on his. "Slow down, Tim. I don't think Romano would operate that way. I don't think he fumbles, you see. As you said, boom, boom. But what about Tony? How would he have felt about it? There was something Patti said this afternoon—everybody connected with *Celebration* was great friends until they realized they might have a very good picture. Then they began quarrelling. Tony advised her to keep out of it."

"Out of what?"

"The quarrels, but between whom? I wish I knew." She gave Tim the proof of the *Celebration* ad to read while she picked up her calls from the service. Marks had left a number at which she could reach him all evening.

Tim said the only name familiar to him was Cardova. He moistened his lips and added, "Actually, Julie, I only know him through a friend of a friend. He wouldn't remember me, that's for sure."

"Okay," Julie said, annoyed at his sudden reluctance to seek out the young director. "I'll try and get to Patti again." She started to dial the number the detective had left for her.

"Marks?" Tim asked.

"Yes."

"You're going to dish out the whole story to him—so he can hold open house for the entire New York press?"

"It's my story," Julie said.

"And my job that's on the line. We're collaborators, sweetheart. Remember? *Our Beat*?"

It took Julie less than one second to recover. "Then get the hell out of here and start collaborating. I don't care how many removes you are from Cardova. We need his story of what went into making *Celebration*."

THIRTY-SIX

M ARKS RANG THE BELL three times, paused and rang three times again, probably waking the entire building, but it was an arrangement they had both thought wise. He wanted something, Julie thought. He didn't come to bear the gift of information. Not at this hour, if ever. His step was heavy on the stairs and the day's growth of beard was dark on his chin and jaws. In the apartment, he lifted his head and inhaled the aroma of coffee. He put a black letter case on the floor alongside the chair he sank into. Before Julie had poured her own coffee he had drunk most of his. When she marveled that he could drink it so hot, he said, "I have a corrugated gullet," and accepted another cup.

He lit a cigarette, reached for the letter case and drew from it a plastic-covered single sheet of typing which he handed to Julie. "I never promised you a rose garden," he said. It was her article on Butts. "Now look at the back."

Julie turned it over and read an agreement hand-written in block letters:

> I, Morton Butts, promise to pay Tony Alexander ten percent of the gross income from the Garden of Roses during my occupancy. The books will be audited twice a year by an accountant agreed to by both of us.

It was signed with the looped signature through which the t's were crossed with one long dash. It was dated the day of Alexander's death.

"Where did you find it?" Julie asked.

Marks took another plastic folder from the case, this one containing a *Tony Alexander Says...* envelope. It was addressed:

Morton Butts
Garden of Roses Ballroom
Amsterdam Av.
NY, NY

"That's Tony's handwriting," Julie said.

Marks nodded. "Butts got it in this morning's mail—no street number, no ZIP code, therefore delayed. What do you make of it?"

"Tony didn't sign it, for one thing."

"And it looks now like he went out to the hall chute and mailed it himself soon after Butts left him."

"He wanted to get rid of it," Julie said. "He wanted no part of Butts' proposition."

"That's what it looks like."

"Why would Butts show it to you at all now? Why wouldn't he eat it first? I mean he came to me so concerned that my article not fall into the hands of an evil doer. It was the agreement written on the back that he must have been most concerned about."

"Well, he has fallen into the hands of evil doers, no question of that. We were there this morning when this arrived for him." He put the two pieces of possible evidence away. "The day he started to register his contestants the mob moved in on him. When we found out the mob's interest, we also moved in and leaned on him—on the theory that under pressure from them, he might have set Alexander up for his killer and then travelled to Brother Joseph's temple like clockwork to establish his own alibi: the precision of his arrival at the hour of witnessing has always bugged me."

"When you say 'the mob,' are you talking about drugs?" Julie asked.

"No. It's a different syndicate. I'm talking about the old protection racket with a weekly collection. It's the protectors who informed him of his drug problems: they guaranteed no interference from the pushers. He bought the protection. I might have done the same thing myself in his position."

"I wonder if they moved in before or after my interview with him," Julie said.

"Is it important to you?" Marks asked blandly.

"Maybe.... I can almost feel sorry for him...the Mafia. Phillips' suicide must have shaken him badly, the one man he really trusted; and then crashing into Tony at the mayor's party..."

"Whom he didn't trust?"

"More importantly, I think, who wouldn't have trusted him. Butts was once a preacher called Jeremiah Fox. He did a lot of baptizing in Tony's home town and got into trouble. He was Tony's enemy, Tony was his."

"Excuse me, Julie, but does it strike you that Butts' long-range plans could be to set up a religious center at the Garden?"

"Oh, yes," Julie said, realizing how close to this conjecture she had come herself. "Of course that's what it's all about. He's got five years to make it, and if he has a congregation by then, is the city going to evict him? No way. He starts out with the 'dance away the habit' scheme. Lots of publicity on drug rehabilitation, a television crusade—and that's where the money is. I could write the scenario. And Tony probably did."

"So the ten percent was an attempted bribe? And the rush to Brother Joseph's was nothing more than Butts kibitzing his competition. He said it this morning: the last place in the world where he wanted to be conspicuous was Brother Joseph's. But after Alexander's death, he had no choice."

Julie was trying to imagine how Tony would have felt, meeting Jeremiah Fox at the mayor's party.... The eager, fearful Fox, prancing after him, begging him not to hurt his chance at the ministry again, and all the while, Tony's mind would have been on Patti Royce. And Morielli? Then came Eleanor's silent phone calls, and Fran's alarm about Eleanor and the gun, his own sea of troubles. "I'm thinking about Tony mailing that rotten piece of paper himself," she said. "He simply had too much worrying him at the time to deal with Butts. I can see him in my mind's eye—getting up from his desk, stuffing the paper into an envelope, addressing it, and lumbering out to the mail drop with it just to get it off his mind."

"So," Marks said, "we have Alexander returning to the office from the party with a man in tow whom he considered a damn nuisance at the moment. And yet he tried to detain him, if Butts is telling the truth—and I think he is in this instance—the family phone calls, then someone of whom he is afraid, to whom he says, 'I'll be here.' He would detain Butts if he could—safety in numbers? But Butts, having got as far as he could with Alexander, took off. He hasn't said it, but Alexander's fear probably made him jittery himself.

"One of the things the inspector keeps hammering at is why Alexander would open the office door to someone of whom he was that afraid. Now we see he not merely opened the door, but went into the hall and back again. It's probably irrelevant whether he left the door open or not. Did he carry a revolver at this point?"

"Yes," Julie said. "He took it out of the copy box the minute Butts left him."

"And kept it within reach from then on. So how did his assailant get hold of it?"

"By drawing his own gun first," Julie suggested.

Marks was staring at her. "Go on."

"Maybe that wasn't necessary," she amended. "Tony wanted something terribly and he must have thought that someone was about to deliver it to him. It's possible that they both had to examine it. Or that Tony needed to use his hands to get it out of a container."

"And what was in the container?"

"I'm pretty sure it was pornographic film of Patti Royce," Julie said and then immediately backed off again. "I shouldn't say that, Lieutenant. It's guesswork all the way down the line."

"But educated guesswork. You didn't pick up on my saying we thought the mob might have wanted Alexander set up for his killer. So it didn't surprise you, did it?"

"Not really."

"Then you know that Patti Royce is Mafia owned."

"Ron Morielli?"

"His sister may also own a piece. And you may be onto something with the porn film bit, but that's all I'm going to say about it for now."

"I'll bet the sister and Patti did a lesbian turn-on at the Tripod," Julie said.

Marks sighed deeply. "You are over-educated." He rubbed out the cigarette. "I have a big favor to ask of you, Julie. I'm asking you to go no further with your own investigations."

"Why?"

"I'll be honest with you. It was one thing when the two women were prime suspects. But as things are now, you could do us more harm than good. We need time and space. We can't move in like a free-wheeling amateur could. What we do, we've got to make stick."

"I'm sorry, Lieutenant Marks, but I can't stop now. I have an assignment from the newspaper I work for. They're paying me to do the job I'm doing."

Marks flushed and a little white outline became visible around his lips. "We can't spare the men to protect you, Julie."

"I'm not expecting you to. I'm not a witness to anything."

"All right," Marks said. "It's up to you. But I'm going to tell you something I didn't intend to until now: the mob moved in on Butts and his marathon dance not because they saw him registering contestants, but because that's one of Sweets Romano's enterprises—the protection racket. It's the mark of an old time gangster. You set Butts up for him with your phone call asking about the Garden of Roses."

THIRTY-SEVEN

MARKS HAD ONCE AGAIN made it impossible for her to sleep. It did not help to try to deny his information. It did not work to tell herself that Romano was above the petty strong-arm gangsterism of the protection racket. Or that he would not take advantage of an inquiry that came from her. And the hypocrisy of saying he admired Butts' quixotic war on drugs was the most disillusioning. As though illusions about Mafiosi were allowed.

The real betrayer she should be concerned with was herself. No, that was excessive, though what it was an excess of she wasn't certain. She was feeling sorry for Butts, that much was clear; and that was better than feeling sorry for herself. Only when she made up her mind to visit Butts again in the morning was Julie able to get through to her mantra and ease herself into sleep with the remembered, repetitive sound of the sea.

HE SHOOK HER HAND vigorously and proclaimed himself delighted that she had come to see him again. The carpenters were gone, the painters had come. He took her into the arena with the dance run circling them. "I've decided against the strobe lighting," he said. "It's not supposed to look grand or glamorous. Nothing more than adequate—and safe. The whole character of the dance marathon is in its intimacy, people sharing a dance for survival." She could now detect a kind of desperation in his hype, but there was courage in it also. He turned her around to see where rows of seats that looked to have been salvaged in the demolition of an old movie house were tiered on platforms.

"How many seats?"

"Two hundred. Not allowed to have more." He shrugged resignedly. "It's the comfort facilities; we need them all for the contestants and I can't afford to install more."

"How many contestants?"

"We closed out at four hundred. Except for standbys. Are you surprised at the number?"

Julie shook her head.

"Shall we go to the office? It's more comfortable than here. No paint. Can't afford that either. Oh, I'm not complaining. I'm blessed in having got this far without my poor friend Jay to guide me."

In the office where the clutter had become monumental, Butts removed a stack of handbills from a chair so that Julie could sit down. He gave her one of the handbills. It advertised the television kick-off with several name personalities scheduled to take part.

"Quite a roster," Julie said.

"There's still room for you aboard—if you've changed your mind."

"I understand my article showed up after all."

"Yes," he said, and thought for a few seconds before saying, "I can't offer you what I offered Tony Alexander, of course..."

"Neither expected nor wanted," Julie said, "but I think I know why you made it to Tony—so that he wouldn't interfere with the resurrection of the Reverend Jeremiah Fox."

The smile he gave her was like that of a little boy, and he gathered his fist at his breast, a submissive, religious gesture. "You can't know, Mrs. Hayes, the thrill you have given me, saying that name out loud. No matter whether you mean to do good or evil to me now, I won't forget just hearing you say the name."

Julie felt uncomfortable. Power was not her thing. "I don't intend to do evil, Mr. Butts."

"Nobody does except the devil and them he gets possession of. I don't think Mr. Alexander did, but he was frightened and that frightened me, and that's what makes people do bad things to one another."

"Are you speaking of last week or something that happened long ago in Albion, Ohio?"

"Of the night he died, the night I ran away and left him to die. If I'd stayed with him, he might be alive today."

"Or you might both be dead."

"I don't justify myself," Butts said. "I don't believe in self-justification, but I do wonder what he'd have done to thwart my plans for the Garden of Roses if he had lived. I mention it because I am vulnerable if you decide to take advantage."

"I have no such intention, Mr. Butts."

"Then I am much beholden to you. Do you mind if I ask how you heard about Jeremiah Fox?"

"Some old newspapers, some old actors. I know you saved Jay Phillips from an awful mess and probably tried to help him with his problem."

"I can't really say I did that, Mrs. Hayes. I did baptize him, satisfying the girl's parents of his repentance, but in all honesty I must say I felt she should've been the repentant one. Very precocious."

Oh, men, Julie thought. She said, "And I know that you and Tony traded accusations."

"I never heard anything so vicious described so politely. I didn't know him as Tony Alexander, Mrs. Hayes. Or if I heard the name it wasn't the one I remembered him by...not till I met him again the night he was going to die."

"And I know about the baby," Julie said.

"What do you know?"

"That you accidentally drowned it."

Butts doubled his fists and pounded them on his knees. "That just plain isn't so. That baby was on the verge of death when he was put into my hands. His father wanted a miracle. I wanted one. I needed one, and I prayed for one. But the Lord wanted that baby and he took him right out of my hands. I stood accused and the loudest of my accusers was the young reporter who led the charge when they ran me out of town.

"It destroyed my ministry. It destroyed my religion. I called myself God's fool after that. I signed on with a circus as its chaplain, and doubled as a clown. I've been on the fringes of show business ever since.''

"Which eventually brought you back into contact with Jay Phillips,'' Julie said.

"A few years ago when I brought a mini-circus to the vest pocket parks of New York.''

"I don't really see where Tony could have hurt you very much at this date,'' Julie said.

"He said that himself. He asked me what I thought he could do. But when you are as badly damaged as I am, Mrs. Hayes, you are like an animal that never gets over its fear of the broom. When he put together your article and my takeover of the Garden, I was sure he would once more destroy me. You must not mock me in this or I may fall again from grace. I have promised the Lord that if my faith is restored I will build Him a new temple, and that is my true plan for the Garden of Roses.''

"Okay,'' Julie said. "Let me know when you're ready to break it to the press.''

"I would show you the blueprints,'' he said, almost perking up to his old self. Then he flattened out again. "But the fact is, they've been stolen from me . . . and I may never be able to use them anyway.''

Stolen by Romano's minions? Julie thought so. "I'm sorry,'' she said, and decided that while it might be good for her soul to admit the true nature of her regrets, it would not speed the little minister's recovery of his faith.

THIRTY-EIGHT

JULIE ARRIVED at the office to learn that a number of people were looking for her, including Tom Hastings, the executive editor.

"Tim went down to see him," Alice said.

"Great." A story without much content had run well back in the morning papers. But the tagline read that according to police sources a break in the case was expected soon. "How long since Tim went downstairs?"

"A half hour. And Duggan called you from the Sunday desk. He wants to know if he can have the Patti Royce story by tonight. With pictures."

"Yet," Julie added.

"And someone's been calling you every few minutes. She won't leave her name or number."

"Any idea who?"

"I think it's her."

"Who's her?" Julie snapped.

"Miss Royce."

"I'm sorry I snapped," Julie said.

"Why should you be any different from everybody else this morning?"

Julie went to her desk and began making notes on the love story of Tony Alexander and Patti Royce. She saw no point in rushing to Hastings' office now, not with Tim there that long ahead of her. Better to stay close and hope for Patti Royce's phone call. If it was Patti Royce.

"The police are going through the building with a man's picture," Alice said. "They're asking if anybody's seen him, especially the night of Tony's death. Tim says it's the owner of the Turkish bath where he and Tony used to go."

"The name is Ron Morielli. Mean anything to you?"

"No."

Julie glanced at the celebrity file. It remained under quarantine. Or else the police had forgotten about it. She went back to her notes. Photos. She called Advertising to see if they still had the art work for *Celebration*. They hadn't. But a rating had come in for the picture. R, for restricted. Or for Romano, if you saw it that way. Someone on the movie desk explained that there might be two versions, one of which they fired back to the censors to meet certain objections. From the movie desk she also got a still of Patti Royce. She got another break in that Michael Dorfman was out of town; she persuaded his secretary to allow her to use the photograph of Patti from *Autumn Tears*. Alice arranged the pick-up.

But in the end, she simply could not do the article. Not enough facts were in place. She called Duggan and told him where she was with it.

"Here's what you do, Julie: write it the way you think it will go. Then edit as you have to. I'll hold till the last minute."

"How come the hurry all of a sudden, Mr. Duggan?"

"I've been around long enough to know by the smell when a story's getting ripe."

TIM CAME INTO the office looking as though he'd have backed out if he'd seen her in time. "I had to tell him what we have, Julie. I figured you were in a bind so it was up to me."

"Does he still want to see me?"

"I told him you were probably on that Royce interview, which he agreed was pretty big stuff."

"Yeah."

"I had to do it, Julie," he shouted.

"Okay! What happened with Cardova?"

"He's in Rome, Italy."

"Since when?"

"What is this? An inquisition? Yesterday. And I went to the Tripod this morning to see what I could get for you there. It's closed."

"Everybody's getting out of town, right?"

"Julie, the two specials covering Tony's murder are coming up in ten minutes. What do we give them? I promised Hastings."

"What we have," Julie said, "but nothing that we don't have. Just remember, the porn film angle came out of my head, and if that broke without proof, Patti Royce could sue the *Daily* into bankruptcy."

"But that's the big thing, Julie. In a few hours that could be the only exclusive we have left. I mean the police are onto the Tripod angle. I want something out of this for the column."

"And I want those few hours, Tim, even if we have to lock the door. Ask the legal department, if you're so anxious. They're supposed to be watching over us."

"It has been rumored..." Tim said tentatively, as though composing aloud. "No. How's this? 'The police will neither confirm nor deny that film of questionable taste....' Oh shit. That sounds literary."

"You are ambitious, aren't you?"

"I can taste it."

Julie swung around to Alice. "Why doesn't she call, whoever she is? Why didn't she leave a number?" Then: "Alice, do *you* have a number for Patti Royce?"

"I have a number where Tony could be reached in an emergency. I never used it."

"Let's have it," Julie said. Meanwhile she looked up Royce in the phone book. She found a likely number but when she dialed it, the operator came on the line and said that it had been changed to an unlisted number. Julie dialed the number Alice gave her. A man's voice: a soft "hello." Julie asked if she might speak to Miss Royce.

"Who's this?"

Julie broke the connection.

"If a man answers, hang up, right?" Tim said.

Julie nodded. She was trying to decide whether or not the voice was familiar. She couldn't.

Tim went down to intercept the special correspondents. Julie worked on the Sunday magazine feature. She jumped every time the phone rang. It was getting on toward Alice's lunchtime. At twenty past twelve the call came. Julie signalled Alice to stay on the line.

It was Patti. "I need help, sweetie."

"Where are you?"

"I'm at a public phone on West Seventy-second Street, but I'll come to you if you say where. Not Forty-fourth Street, and not your newspaper office."

"Okay. Go to my house on Sixteenth Street." She gave her the number. "I'll leave now and I'll be waiting for you in the vestibule."

Julie waited for an hour downstairs at Sixteenth Street. She went up then and called the office. No word there from Patti. She worked on the article, marking every few minutes while another hour passed. The stillness of the house seemed profound, accented by the chirping of a solitary sparrow in the ailanthus tree at the rear of the building.

Reluctantly, she called Lieutenant Marks.

THIRTY-NINE

"PLAIN COMMON SENSE would tell you they're not going to harm the chick about to lay golden eggs," Marks said.

"Even if she could testify against Morielli?"

"There's a difference between *could* and *would*, Julie."

"So you won't do anything, is that it? You asked me to cease and desist. But what was I supposed to do when she said she needed help: tell her to get lost?"

"You might have suggested she call the police. We're putting out a thirteen-state alarm for Morielli. I hope we get him in a hurry and that we have enough to hold him on. When that happens I think she'll surface. Stop worrying."

"Yeah," Julie said. "Thanks."

She called the city newsroom and passed the word to the specials that a thirteen-state alarm was going out for Ron Morielli. Then she looked up the address of Patti Royce's agent.

FORTY

"JULIE HAYES to see Mr. Macken," she said, standing tall at the receptionist's desk.

"Do you have an appointment?"

"Yes," she lied.

She waited on an ornamental iron bench that must have made an impression on a lot of bottoms. The building was a converted hat factory with fancy metal work and plaster columns topped with art nouveau pediments.

Macken came out almost at once, as though to make up for the phone calls of hers he had ignored that long time ago when she'd wanted to make her first inquiry about Patti Royce. He looked stylish and successful: sculpted dark hair, small grey eyes, dimpled chin that jutted, and a tight dark suit. He held her hand longer than necessary, leading her into his inner office. "Patti told me you were doing a story on her. How can I help?"

His secretary gave Julie a flash smile.

"You can help me find her, first thing," Julie said. "We arranged to meet but she didn't show up." Before sounding the alarm she hoped to learn where Macken's loyalty was. The office didn't tell her much about Creative Talent, Inc. From where she sat with him on ice cream parlor chairs at a porcelain topped table, it looked like a one-man operation.

"That's twice now we've stood you up, you might say. I'm sorry about that."

"Three times if you want to count," Julie said. "Mr. Morielli and his sister broke up our interview yesterday."

"A difficult man," Macken murmured and Julie knew he wasn't the kind who volunteered.

"Was he the one who chose you as Patti's agent?"

He looked at her as though he couldn't believe her naiveté.

"I might as well put my question directly, Mr. Macken:
How much did you know about Ron Morielli and Patti
when you took her on?"

"I never know more than I want to know. I know him
only as Patti's manager and one of the producers of a film
called *Celebration*. I agreed with Mr. Alexander that if she
was handled right—and if the picture was handled right—
nobody connected with it would ever go hungry again, as
Scarlett O'Hara said. It was my idea to put her into daytime television, just to keep her busy until the distribution
was set and the picture released."

"It was a long time between engagements for Patti," Julie said.

Macken made a noncommital sound. He was doodling on
the white table-top, a female head of comic strip beauty.
"She told you that she'd been a child star?"

"We talked about it, but we got cut off before we got to
Morielli."

Macken leaned back and played with the pencil for a
minute. "She told me once he was a Humphrey Bogart figure to her. Better not use that until you check it out with her.
And Morielli."

"How about Tony? What kind of a figure was he?"

"Daddy-bear," he said deep in his throat.

That one checked out, and she began to feel that Macken
really didn't know much about the people around *Celebration*. Blind, because he refused to look. "You know Tony's
contribution to the picture, don't you? He wrote the story.
David Clemens is a pseudonym."

"Doesn't mean much. It's Cardova's picture. He'll be
right up there with Zeffirelli and Zinneman. I wish I had
him in my stable." He was pencilling a mustache on the female profile. "Why don't you wait for Patti to come to you,
Mrs. Hayes? She'll come, don't worry. She gets absent-
minded, but there isn't a more sentimental gal in show
business, and to her you're Tony's alter ego."

"How does that make Morielli feel about me?"

Macken gave an enormous shrug.

"She tried all morning to reach me by phone, Mr. Macken, and when she did reach me, she said she needed help. I gave her my address and went home to wait for her. She never showed up."

"Today's Wednesday, isn't it? She's supposed to be home learning her lines." He put the pencil away in an inside pocket and called out to his secretary to bring him a phone.

She brought the phone, plugged it in, poked out the number for him and handed over the one-piece instrument.

Julie heard the signal, then the click of someone's picking up, but no voice.

"Patti, is that you?" Macken said. "No games, Patti…"

But no response came from the other end and he hung up, then called another number. "Let me talk to Ron. It's Ted Macken." At the end of that call, he told Julie what she already knew: "The police are looking for him." He seemed genuinely shocked.

"But not for Patti," Julie said.

"He'll take her with him, if he's on the run. Believe me, he isn't going to let her go. And I'm going to be in trouble with Procter and Gamble."

"Is that why Tony was going to marry her—to get her away from him?"

"That crossed my mind once or twice. Mrs. Hayes, I don't have the answers to your questions. And if I had them, I wouldn't give them to you now without consulting my lawyer."

"Just let me bounce off a couple more of them: Somewhere in there Patti made a porn film, didn't she?"

He made a face: what difference? But he said nothing.

"I'll bet her part in the soap opera is nice and wholesome, right?"

"You don't watch daytime television, do you? There are no nice, wholesome parts. She's the hospital lay. Calling all doctors."

"Oh," Julie said.

"Where was she when she phoned you?" Macken asked.

"At a public phone on Seventy-second Street."

"That's crazy. She lives right there. Somebody's in the place. Somebody picked up the phone just now."

There was a lot of street to Seventy-second, east and west. Then it occurred to Julie, the most famous address, east *or* west: "The Dakota?"

He nodded.

"Does Morielli have a key?"

"He owns the apartment."

"So maybe he's hiding out there," Julie said.

"If you were looking for him, where would you look first?"

"I see what you mean," Julie said. "Then who's picking up the phone? How about his sister, Mrs. Conti?"

"She and her husband flew down to Key West this morning—to rest up for the opening."

"Yeah," Julie said. Then: "I didn't know she had a husband."

"In emergencies," Macken said.

FORTY-ONE

JULIE WALKED THROUGH Madison Square after she left Macken's office. There was a wind and the air was clear, and the trees had managed to drop a few leaves of dappled yellow and red among the shrivelled browns and muddy greens. She was closer to home than to anywhere else she wanted to go. She felt very much alone. Not afraid exactly, but vulnerable. And curiously, a kind of ache for Tony had come upon her.

She called the office and the answering service. No one was making immediate demands on her. The story had not yet broken: the midnight edition. She could drop out for the rest of the day and not be missed. Maybe for days...

With a cup of tea in hand, she replayed the tape she had made after Romano's call. "Given what you know of my filmic and photographic interests..." If there was pornographic film of Patti, he knew it. He probably owned it. If that were so, Tony ought to have known he wasn't going to get it. Perhaps there was no such film. Nor ever had been. In which case, *Celebration* was principally at issue. Art is never pornography, Miss Julie. He claimed to want the picture protected as a work of art, untouched by scandal. All of this seemed to put him and Tony on the same side. Except that one of them was dead.

FORTY-TWO

"He ought to have been an investigative reporter," Fran said. She pressed the soil around a young plant, and gave the plastic pot a little pat as she set it among the others on a tray above the bench. "I'm glad you told me," she said of the Tripod connection and the producers of *Celebration*. "I suppose it's all bound to get full press coverage?"

"I'm afraid so," Julie said. "It will break tonight in the *Daily*. It was Tim's scoop, really, and he consulted with Mr. Hastings. I wish they'd included me, but I wasn't there in time. I'd have tried to hold back a while longer."

"Thank you for that," Fran said.

Julie thought of telling the truth, that it was for Patti Royce's sake as much as for the perpetuation of the Tony Alexander legend that she'd wanted to hold back. Tony would become a legend if Fran had her way: the columnist who would infiltrate the mob, if necessary by marriage, if necessary breaking up his own marriage, to conduct the exposé he wanted. In a little while Fran might even come to believe it. It was not a moment of truth on either of their parts.

"All his life," Fran said, going to the front of the shop with Julie, "he would dig himself into a situation where the only way out was by explosion. And when the dust cleared, he had his story. Ask Jeff."

"I will. I'll be talking to him soon. Fran, how did Tony feel about pornography?"

"That it was a form of perversion. He was a puritan, you know. Very straight. I suppose that's hard for you to believe."

"No." It had nothing to do with the Tripod. Nor with his making passes. They were Tony's kind of tribute.

Fran took a dark, velvety red rose from the refrigerator and laced it through the buttonholes of Julie's raincoat. She unlocked the shop door. Two black-and-white but mostly dirt-grey cats were waiting. "What do I do about them? Eleanor's refugees. She goes back to school tomorrow, thank God. Look at them. They expect to be fed."

"Better feed them," Julie said.

THE MIDNIGHT EDITION broke the story of Tony Alexander and Patti Royce, former child star coming back the hard way, via the massage parlor and a sleeper film, *Celebration*. Patti's one-time boss and lover, the owner of the Tripod Turkish Baths, Ron Morielli, was being sought by the police for questioning in Alexander's murder. Miss Royce was thought by the police to be in seclusion.

One-time boss and lover, Julie thought. If Patti was twenty-one years old, how long ago could one-time be? The chick expected to lay the golden eggs, Marks had said, and therefore safe. Or could it be that the police were holding her to bait a trap for Morielli? Marks had seemed so very sure of himself. But that was how police had to sound.

SHE WAS OUTSIDE the television studio in the early morning. So were a lot of reporters. Patti didn't show. The taping schedule of *Forgotten Splendor* was a shambles. Actors in later-scheduled segments arrived, hair tousled, scripts in hand.

Julie spotted Ted Macken getting out of a cab. She didn't try to get near him, but from those who did word spread that Patti was suffering from fatigue and nervous exhaustion. She went to the shop on Forty-fourth Street. She felt utterly safe, as though all the action had gone somewhere else and left her. Or as though she was waking from a nightmare and wanted back in instead of out of it. She called Sweets Romano.

As was customary between them, she left her name and he called right back. "I proposed to phone you this morning, Miss Julie. So much, it would seem, has gone awry. I shall send Michael for you. Will you come?''

"Mr. Romano, I'm worried about Patti Royce."

"I understand," he said and hung up.

FORTY-THREE

THE LAME DRIVER, Michael, scuttled around the limousine to open the door for her. "I'm glad to see you again, Miss Julie."

She wished she could say the same. "Thank you, Michael."

She rode up Eighth Avenue seeing it even a few shades greyer than normal through the tinted glass. Was the glass bullet-proof? She supposed so. Although Romano claimed never to leave his home she knew he sent the car for a variety of associates to meet with him, and having once seen a carload of men he called his "Board" she ought to have been able to accept him at police value. He himself enjoyed suggesting to her his villainous career. And yet he reigned, undisturbed by the Law, in a vast and beautifully appointed penthouse in the east Seventies.

Michael opened the panel and said over his shoulder, "Would you like to go through the park, Miss Julie? It's a beautiful day."

From where she sat she couldn't tell.

Alberto, Romano's young man of many tasks, took her up in the private elevator, and Romano himself opened the door to her. An aging cherub—if cherubs ever aged—the round soft face, pink cheeks and very blue eyes; but the skin was beginning to pinch.

"How kind of fortune to take time out from all its dismal deeds to bring us together! Come in, Miss Julie." He stepped back and tucked his hands into the pockets of a blue velvet jacket. He ought to have known she would not offer to shake hands, well aware that he could not bear to touch, however fond he was of a person. He had once called himself the ultimate voyeur. "Shall we go and sit in the company of our old friend, Vuillard?"

They passed from the foyer into the sky-lit living room and took the same chairs they had sat in before, facing the Vuillard painting of an old man.

"There will be coffee presently," Romano said. "So: the very exploitation both of us would have avoided has occurred—all the nasty little liaisons of pleasure revealed to the greedy public."

"It was not my story," Julie said.

"I observed. Never mind. The film will speak for itself and be heard when all is hushed in Babel."

"Mr. Romano, I'm worried about Patti Royce."

"So you proposed to tell me on the phone. This is much better: one never knows with whom one is sharing a private line. I should have thought that worry about Patti Royce was an excess of charity, but perhaps I'm wrong. I have never been an astute judge of women. But as a distinguished president once said—I believe it was of art in his case—I know what I like."

"Do you know where she is?"

"As a matter of fact, I do. You will have coffee?"

"No, thank you."

"Ah, but you will." And he turned her attention toward the door then opening. Through it came Patti Royce, bearing, with a total lack of grace, a tray with service for three.

Romano leaped to his feet and took the tray from her. "What a disastrous proposal this was!" he said of Patti's serving the coffee.

Patti came and seated herself on the arm of Julie's chair. She folded a purple satin robe over her knees. "Don't be mad because I didn't call you, sweetie. I wanted to but he said I'd better not." The robe kept slipping open all the way up to her thighs.

Julie felt numb. The relief she might have expected was entirely missing. What grew in her was a feeling of foolishness. Then she thought of Tony and anger took over.

Romano, having set the tray on a table near his chair, was watching her, interpreting her every expression. "Please don't despise your own kindness, or for that matter, Mr. Alexander's chivalry. He was a most unlikely knight and his armor didn't fit very well. But let me say, Miss Julie, his cause is won, his dream of fair women quite safe. It is of no significance that I do not share his vision."

Julie took a deep breath. "Are we talking about a pornographic film Patti made before *Celebration*?"

Patti bit her lip and then said, "I had to make a living some way. How was I to know anything good was ever going to happen to me again?"

Romano clucked disapproval. "I am disappointed. I'd have thought there was no need to be explicit. No one will ever see that obscenity again except Romano—and I very much doubt that he will." He looked at the actress with an expression of supreme distaste. He poured Julie a small cup of coffee and brought it to her, dispatching Patti from the arm of the chair.

Patti headed straight for the chair under the Vuillard facing them.

"Not there! You must take her out of here with you, Miss Julie. She is a thing of beauty to me only in film, and no joy whatsoever."

Patti seated herself on the floor at Julie's feet.

"What happened after you called me yesterday?" Julie asked.

"Michael was waiting to offer our services," Romano answered for her. "It had occurred to me that rarely in her life had she been given a choice worth the choosing. I was wrong. It was a battle of equal wits between her and Morielli. Even with Alexander on her side, she couldn't win."

"I didn't want to win," Patti said. "I wanted to run."

"Then now is the time!" Romano made shooing motions with his delicate little hands. "Gather your clothes and don't leave anything behind you. You are not to return, you understand. Romano is not a proper instructor for someone who cannot learn."

"I couldn't come back if I wanted to," Patti said. "I don't even know where I am."

"You do see what I mean, Miss Julie," he said when Patti had left the room.

"May I ask a question directly, Mr. Romano?"

"So long as you don't expect a direct answer." He chortled and poured his own coffee.

"Tony wanted the film, didn't he? To make sure it never got out to the public?"

"What difference does it make at this point?"

"I want to know why he died and who killed him."

"I suppose that is important," Romano said. "But I assure you this 'property' of which you speak was in my possession for many months. My financing of the picture was conditional on its delivery—master print, negative, and all copies—something of which, you will perhaps understand, Mr. Alexander could never have been certain."

"So Tony didn't know you had it."

"I didn't say that. In truth, I don't know whether he knew it or not. He was not likely to have trusted me any further than he trusted Morielli."

"That was too bad," Julie said.

"Very unfortunate."

IN THE CAB, on which Julie insisted instead of the limousine, Patti said, "When I first got there I thought it was like paradise and I could live there forever. Then I got the creeps. I was so glad when I found out you were coming. Do you know who he reminds me of? Jay Phillips in a way—something soft and awful."

"Patti, where's Ron Morielli?"

"Mr. Romano says the police will have to extradite him from South America if they want him."

"They do."

"Does that mean he killed Tony?"

"It means they think so. Where was he the night Tony was killed?"

"He was supposed to be at the Tripod—you know . . ."

"I know," Julie said.

"The police kept asking me why I said *supposed*, and I always told them that's just the way I talk. But if he's gone, I'm glad. See, that's why I went so easy with Mr. Romano's man. I've always needed somebody to protect me."

"I understand," Julie said. "If Ron wasn't at the Tripod when he was supposed to be there, where was he?"

"I don't know, Julie. Honest. He kept promising Tony to bring him that dirty old picture, but I don't know for a fact."

"Okay. When did Tony find out about the picture?"

"Well, he thought it was so terrible me working at the Tripod: so I told him about the picture. He said I was a white slave, which I didn't like much."

"Patti, someone's in your apartment. Who?"

"Two men Ron gave the key to. They're supposed to be protecting me. But I'm more scared of them than anybody, and when I got a chance I grabbed my *Forgotten Splendor* bag and ran."

Which, Julie realized, was where the purple dressing gown had come from.

"Julie, do you mind if we go straight to the Ninth Avenue Studios? I'm late, I know, but you could give them some story while I get into costume. Then you and I could finish the interview when I'm not needed on the set."

IN THE LATE AFTERNOON Julie went to the office in the *Daily* building. Alice had prepared three columns of copy that Tim had left for Julie's approval. In the quiet after Alice had gone she wrote the article for the Sunday magazine...any Sunday. She had missed the deadline. She had no idea whether the piece was good or not. It was the best she could do. She remembered all too well sitting in the same setting and starting out, *I never promised you a rose garden*. Her desk had been positioned differently then. Now she stared across the room at the plastic-shrouded celebrity file. She had some new names since she and Marks had consulted it, and the uneasy feeling that the truth as well as Morielli had somehow escaped them.

She decided to break the law. Carefully. She threw back the shroud, trespassed on Alice's desk drawer to find a tweezers and, in the manner Marks had taught her, looked up David Clemens. He was there, in Tony's own hand: "A writer of excellent promise whose trouble is he may have a contract put out on him before he ever has one offered to him.''

She went to the M's. No entry under Morielli. Back to the C's. Conti: no entry. Cardova: ''Eduardo Cardova, a Latin lover type, and a film director of some promise. A sweets darling.''

Tony had written what he meant, she was sure: sweets, as in Sweets Romano. Knowing Romano's phobic voyeurism, she had to wonder if by any chance Cardova was involved in the pornography. She had to wonder, but she didn't have to know.

FORTY-FOUR

IT WAS A FEW DAYS later that Marks reached her by phone. "I think we have Morielli, what's left of him. The head and torso surfaced in waters off Staten Island. The feet are probably down there somewhere in cement." He paused. "Are you there?"

"I'm here."

"This has a way of happening to Romano expendables. I was afraid of it. I wanted to get to him first."

"I wish you had," Julie said.

"Now I want Romano and—Julie—I'll need all the help I can get."

Worldwide Mysteries—keeping you in suspense with award-winning authors.

THE DEAD ROOM—Herbert Resnicow $3.50   ☐
When a murdered man is found in a dead room, an anechoic
chamber used to test stereo equipment, Ed Baer and his son
investigate the virtually impossible crime, and unravel an
ingenious mystery.

MADISON AVENUE MURDER—Gillian Hall $3.50   ☐
A young woman investigates the brutal murder of a successful
art director and comes to understand the chilling flip side of
passionate love . . . and the lowly places to which the highest
ambitions can fall.

LULLABY OF MURDER—Dorothy Salisbury Davis $3.50   ☐
A reporter investigates the murder of a famous New York gossip
columnist and finds herself caught up in a web of hate, deceit
and revenge.

IN REMEMBRANCE OF ROSE—M. R. D. Meek $3.50   ☐
An elderly woman is found dead, victim of an apparent robbery
attempt. But lawyer Lennox Kemp is suspicious and discovers
that facts are scarce and bizarre, leading him to believe that
there is something sinister at play.
Not available in Canada.

Total Amount	$ _____
Plus 75¢ Postage	_____.75
Payment enclosed	$ _____

Please send a check or money order payable to Worldwide Mysteries.

In the U.S.A.	In Canada
Worldwide Mysteries	Worldwide Mysteries
901 Fuhrmann Blvd.	P.O. Box 609
Box 1325	Fort Erie, Ontario
Buffalo, NY 14269-1325	L2A 5X3

Please Print
Name: _____
Address: _____
City: _____
State/Prov: _____
Zip/Postal Code: _____

 WORLDWIDE LIBRARY